*Margaret Yorke*

# SILENT WITNESS

ARROW BOOKS

Arrow Books Limited
3 Fitzroy Square, London W1

An imprint of the Hutchinson Publishing Group

London Melbourne Sydney Auckland
Wellington Johannesburg and agencies
throughout the world

First published in Great Britain by
Hutchinson & Co (Publishers) Ltd,
Arrow edition 1979


Made and printed in Great Britain
by The Anchor Press Ltd
Tiptree, Essex

ISBN 0 09 914880 3

# Contents

To the Dorothies, affectionately

*NOTE*

The village of Greutz, its neighbourhood, and all the characters in this book, are imaginary.

## PART ONE

# Morning

### I

Through the softly-falling snow it came down to the valley, descending the mountain propped like a doll, frozen stiff in its seat. First to see it were the *lehrers*, riding up early on the chair-lift to open the runs, and grizzled Hans Schulz whose days were now spent helping skiers off the lift at Obergreutz. It passed above each of them as they rose. The head lolled against the pole on which the chair hung from its wire hawser; the feet, with skis on, were neatly together on the rail; and one arm was hooked over the bar across the knees. A thick layer of snow covered it, so that it seemed dressed in white. As the men travelling upwards saw it, their shouts shocked those below into some sort of preparation for the end of the macabre journey. Slowly the chair swung downwards: the loaded seat with its rigid burden swinging across the black, shining river until it came to rest on the plank platform of the terminus. The machinery stopped.

There were few to greet the body: the snowcat driver who had not yet mounted the chair; the men who worked the lift; a few visitors out early; and the burgomeister, hastily summoned from his nearby house while at his breakfast, who stood with crumbs still around his whiskers, summoning the concentration to direct what must now be done.

From the balcony of a chalet on the other side of the valley, Dr. Patrick Grant, Fellow of St. Mark's College, Oxford, watched the scene through a pair of binoculars as a small crowd began to gather at the bottom of the chair-lift.

# PART TWO

## Saturday

### I

Snow had fallen every day for three weeks, and the atmosphere in the village of Greutz, high in the Austrian Alps, had become charged with foreboding. Increasing masses on the mountain peaks constantly threatened skiers with restrictions because of avalanche risk; frequent closures of the road over the pass, at first lightly thought of by recently-arrived holiday-makers, now brought a sense of claustrophobia : one could be cut off, imprisoned in the village, miss one's connection home, and be badly inconvenienced. But no thought of anything worse entered the heads of the visitors who had come to Greutz, until one of them disappeared.

The village was long and straggling, a line of shops and chalets that bordered the road leading down from the high mountain pass. Most of the chalets in the main street were hotels or *pensions*, but a track past the church, with its onion dome and spiky spire, continued to a few private dwellings used at weekends by people who came from as far away as Munich. By the side of the road ran the river, normally black and fast-flowing but torpid now, the boulders that studded it wearing tall white hats of snow. A roofed wooden bridge crossed it, and here, in an open space where the tennis courts were in summer, the ski-school met, behind the clinic and the bank.

At the end of the main street, where the road wound along the side of the valley to Kramms, past the Sportshop Winkler and the chair-lift terminus, a lane branched off up a slope to the Hotel Gentiana. Its position, tucked away from the centre of the village, was much boosted by travel agents because of its seclusion, the benefits of which were sometimes a matter of doubt to weary skiers trudging homewards up the hill at the end of the day with their skis weighing down their shoulders. Only the Red Run ended near the Gentiana, and it was a difficult one; because of the dividing river no other runs connected with its final stages, and only the experienced were advised to tackle the narrow, often icy *piste* which dropped steeply down the side of the mountain through the trees and over a hanging bridge across the river. Sometimes walkers took the trail through the woods, but they seldom climbed far, preferring to follow the easier path on the other side of the river.

The Hotel Gentiana had been owned by the Scholler family for three generations. The original inn, catering mainly for climbers, had panelled walls and ceilings, ornately carved, and creaky floors that sloped at odd angles. A new wing had been added at one side, incorporating a restaurant with huge windows looking up to Obergreutz and beyond to the peak of the Schneiderhorn which had been hidden for days now behind dense, snow-laden clouds. Above the restaurant there were bedrooms, and below, in the cellar, was the Gentiana nightclub with its discotheque. Behind the building was a modern chalet used as an annexe, where the rooms were smaller, barer, and cheaper than those in the main hotel.

At lunch-time the lifts, and even the cable-car from Kramms to Obergreutz, had stopped, for the snow that had been falling steadily all the morning was coming down in a dense white curtain through which all vision was obscured. Only the two short drags on the nursery slopes were working, and a few hardy spirits, hooded and wearing goggles, rode up them to career blindly down at speed, scattering this year's learners who floundered about for a time and then gave up, soaked and depressed, to take themselves off to Ferdy's for hot chocolate or a grog.

In his room on the first floor of the Gentiana annexe, Bernard Walker gazed moodily out at the descending snow. His direct view was of the wall of the main hotel, but by opening the window and putting his head out he could look towards the village and see if the lifts were working; now, however, the snow was falling so heavily that even if they were running they would be invisible. He knew by the silence that they had stopped. That morning, despite the conditions, he had done the Red Run three times. Knees flexed, eyes screwed up behind the double barrier of spectacles and goggles, blue wool cap pulled well over brow and ears, he had side-slipped down the sheer drop from the shoulder of the mountain and then turned to run straight as the *piste* curved in gentle undulations for some two hundred yards before widening into a plateau where the runs divided. Here the *piste* to Kramms led off to the left, and there was a choice of three routes back to Greutz. He had been with his ski-class on the first two trips; they had gone up in the chair-lift to Obergreutz, and there connected with the long anchor drag that hoisted skiers in pairs to the top of the Schneiderhorn and the network of lifts and runs that laced its summit and joined it with other villages on the farther slopes. Coming down, the snow had found its way inside hoods, collars and gloves. Bernard's glasses had steamed up; despite his thick socks and two pairs of gloves his feet and hands were numb, and his legs felt stiff after the long haul on the drag. By the time the class had travelled up for the second time the high anchor lift had been stopped because of the worsening weather; the rest of his group swooped off down the mountain aiming for the friendly fug of Ferdy's bar; only Bernard had returned to the chair-lift for the third time.

At the junction where the runs divided he had paused, tempted to take an easier way down now that he was alone, but his morning's target had been three descents of the Red Run. He did a quick jump turn and took the narrow track, running fast along the twisting *piste*, trusting to luck to find the bumps on which to turn for he could not see them. It was eerily silent coming through the trees; because of their shelter the snow fell less heavily, and as he had the path to himself he could set his own pace without fear of collision. He had been the last person up on the chair-lift, and those in front had taken the easier runs down. It was, he thought, a pity that there was no audience to admire his swinging christies as he came fast out of the wood, went straight over the hanging bridge that crossed the river at this point, and down the final slope, ending with a skidding turn on the steep bank of snow above the lane outside the hotel. The only soul in sight was an old, bent man pulling a sledge along the lane towards the village.

Bernard undid his skis, stood them on end and knocked off the loose snow with his glove. Then he strapped them together, hoisted them on to his shoulder, clambered down the bank and walked round the side of the hotel to the ski-room, where he stacked his skis and sticks in a corner position in the rack.

This done, he debated for a moment his next move. It was twelve o'clock, peak hour in the village bars. Bernard unclipped his boots at the ankles and walked off down the road to Ferdy's. There, the members of his ski-class were grouped round a table with tall glasses before them and an array of empty bottles; it was an advanced class, all men, for at this level few women had the stamina, even if they had the skill, to keep up the pace set by the men; but at the table several girls had joined them, including Fiona Spilman, a tall, pale, wand-like girl with auburn hair who operated the discotheque in the Gentiana nightclub. The air was thick with cigarette smoke and the gently rising steam from damp garments.

'You got down all right, then,' said one of the men as Bernard hovered by their table. No one attempted to make a space for him to join them.

'Rather. I had a splendid run,' Bernard replied in a keen voice. 'Hi there, Fiona.'

Fiona did not answer, and no one else spoke to him. Bernard peered about, looking to see who else was in the bar. A woman in a scarlet sweater sitting alone at a corner table waved to him, and he crossed the room towards her.

'Hullo, Bernard. Sit here, won't you?' Sue Carter invited. She was large and fair, in her early thirties, with blue eyes and the clear complexion of someone who spent much of her time out of doors.

'Sorry, I can't stop, I'm meeting someone,' Bernard said abruptly, and he swung away from her, out of the bar, his cap still on his head.

From Ferdy's he crossed to the Silvretta. In the tea-room, he walked among the tables as if seeking somebody. There were several people from the Gentiana sitting there with drinks, and he paused long enough to greet those he recognised, but with an urgent air. Then he hurried out and went up the road to the self-service store, where he bought a packet of crisps and a bottle of lemonade.

Carrying his purchases in a paper bag, he walked back the way he had so lately come, along the road to the end of the village, up the track again past the main building of the Gentiana into the annexe, and so to his own small room, where he sat on his bed eating his crisps and drinking his lemonade in solitude until it was time for lunch.

And now Bernard stood at his bedroom window wondering how to occupy the rest of the day. After staring gloomily at the snow for a while he picked up his anorak, put it on and went out on to the landing. On the floor above lived Penny Croft, the courier for Hickson's Holidays who had annual block bookings at the Silvretta and the Gentiana. As it was Saturday she was now in Zürich, supervising the departure of today's outgoing guests and collecting the new arrivals. The bus bringing them was due back in Greutz at nine o'clock, but if the snow continued to fall at this rate the road over the pass would soon be blocked again.

Also on the second floor of the annexe was Fiona's room. Every night, or rather, early every morning, Bernard heard her overhead when she came in after her session at the discotheque. Now, pausing at the head of the stairs, he heard a sudden blare of pop music from above and then a peal of female laughter followed by the rumble of a man's voice. He clattered quickly down the stairs in his heavy ski boots, blundered over the short distance separating the annexe from the main hotel, and pushed his way through the glass swing door. Frau Scholler, busy behind the reception desk checking her accounts, saw him pass; he did not look at her. Most of her guests were in the lounge, reading, writing postcards, or playing bridge; there would be a steady and profitable demand for tea, coffee, and later grogs and *gluwein* throughout the afternoon, but if the weather did not soon improve the visitors would grow irritable. Frau Scholler had seen it happen many times before. She sighed, and went on adding up *schillings* upon *schillings* with practised accuracy.

In the lounge, Bernard glanced anxiously round. There might be someone present who would speak to him, demanding the sort of response he could rarely, if ever, give. Bernard had never risen to any occasion, however minor, except when ski-ing. When he was younger, an acquaintance at work had persuaded him, because someone else had dropped out at the last minute, to join a ski-ing party. Bernard, who never knew how to spend his holiday and who at this stage in his life still hoped he might one day achieve human contact of some kind, had gone along. Surprising himself as much as his companions, he had made rapid progress and become the star pupil of his ski-class; taking the sport so seriously gave him an excuse to opt out of late nights, and to build an image for himself. He ski-ed, but he did not dance. His fame on the slopes followed him back to England, and he cultivated it. Each year after that he went to a different resort, alone, so that no one he knew could report upon his social life. At the office he could boast of feats upon the mountain that were genuine, and obscurely hint at subtler personal adventures which were not.

But if bad weather stopped one ski-ing, what else could one do? One must seem busy, or people would expect one to join in their activities. There were all these women about, too many of them unattached and possibly predatory. Bernard shuddered at the thought of them. All that flesh, soft and yielding, even demanding: certainly mysterious. He would not admit that the idea of it fascinated him, even as it repelled.

The lounge, now, seemed safe from female menace. There was no sign of Sue Carter and her friend Liz Morris who had travelled out in the same party the previous weekend. The only fellow Britons to be seen were three other clients of Hickson's Holidays – Francis and Barbara Whittaker and Sam Irwin. Barbara was a smart, striking-looking woman, but she was safely married; Bernard did not see the covert glance she gave him, over her cards, as he entered; it was a swift assessment and dismissal. Sam Irwin had the next room to Bernard's in the annexe; he seemed a quiet man, not given to getting drunk and crashing into bed with groans, or worse, with women, habits which Bernard had encountered in his neighbours in the past, forcing him to stuff his fingers in his ears and hide, child-like, with the bedclothes over his head, shutting out the frightening sounds. Their fourth at the bridge table was Frau Hiller, a widow from Frankfurt, who had come here for the curling but had thus far been frustrated, for no amount of snow-blowing could keep the rink clear.

It would be safe to sit here for a while, where it was more comfortable than in his cell-like room. Bernard would not allow himself the thought that it was a relief not to be sitting in a blizzard on a chair-lift, swinging through the blinding snowfall, or straining all the muscles in his legs twisting his way down the mountain side. He crossed to a shelf which held a row of tattered paperbacks in several languages, studied the titles, and selected one. Then, hanging his anorak over the back of his chair, he settled himself in a corner behind a potted palm and began to read.

## II

Sue Carter, too, was reading, but upstairs, stretched out on her bed, and her book was about Renaissance Italy, for she perpetually struggled to repair gaps in her cultural knowledge. Her friend Liz Morris, with whom she shared a double room in the old timbered part of the Gentiana, was finishing the crossword in the previous weekend's *Sunday Times*. She looked up from time to time to see how Sue was making out with Michelangelo; soon, heavy breathing indicated that the diet was too much after a large lunch : Sue slept.

Liz gave up the puzzle, wrote on a piece of paper in big capitals GONE FOR WALK. MAY CALL AT FERDY'S, and put it under Sue's hairbrush on their shared dressing-table; then she collected her purse, her bright blue anorak and her gloves, and went quietly from the room.

Before going out of the building she looked into the hotel lounge and saw Bernard by his potted palm, deep in *Sons and Lovers*.

Near the window was the bridge four: Barbara Whittaker was as usual dressed like someone pictured in a glossy magazine, today in a gold sweater and pants, with her hair newly rinsed to match. She alone of the guests staying in the Gentiana was unperturbed by the constant bad weather, for she did not ski; she liked, though, to acquire a becoming tan from sitting in the sun or strolling along the mountain paths, and she had done none of that so far. Her husband Francis, a grey-haired, sturdy man who spoke good German, was partnering Frau Hiller, pear-shaped and genial with immense powers of concentration; the fourth member of the table was Sam Irwin, a lean, dark man whom Sue, ever optimistic, had been delighted to find travelling out to Greutz among the band of Hickson's holidaymakers the weekend before.

'Two unattached men! What luck!' she'd said to Liz, seeing Sam and Bernard still left with them and the Whittakers in the bus after its other passengers had all been dropped at different places on the way to Greutz.

'Don't count your chickens,' Liz advised dryly. 'They're both professional bachelors, you mark my words.'

'You, Elizabeth Morris, are an embittered, twisted old has-been,' Sue retorted. 'Maybe they are a trifle shy, but that means nothing. I shall have a go at the dark one, he's prettier.'

So far her efforts had met with no success. Sam Irwin was civil but not chatty; he disappeared after breakfast each day, presumably to ski, was seldom in to lunch, and in the evenings joined the Whittakers, with whom he was soon on friendly terms.

'I'm right, you see,' said Liz. 'He doesn't go for dames. Barbara, being married, makes him feel safe. If he really understood women he'd know she's much more dangerous than we are.'

'You're too cynical by half. I pity you,' Sue sighed.

'You never will learn from past experiences,' said Liz.

She remembered this conversation now as she set off down the road, leaving the bridge players and Bernard, solitary with his book, behind her. There was something about Sam Irwin that puzzled her; he seemed familiar.

The snow eddied round her as she trudged along the lane, the thick flakes swirling. After weeks spent looking forward to blue skies and champagne air this weather was most depressing, but the only thing to do was to make the best of it; at least the hotel was comfortable and the food good, though the company was not exactly scintillating. Perhaps among today's expected guests there would be some lively character or other who would cheer things up. As things were, the ski-ing prospects were poor; Liz did not enjoy groping her way down the sides of mountains in blinding blizzards. She had ski-ed for part of every day until today, but this morning she had rebelled against another two-hour stint with her ski-class, coming snail-like down the White Run pausing on the way to do boring exercises every hundred yards or so. She was a moderate skier, but she did not go fast and she hated the regimentation of the ski-school; Sue had less experience and lacked the courage to leave the sheltering wing of the *ski-lehrer*, so that Liz, for want of a companion to ski with, was forced to join a class.

That morning she had walked with Sue to the ski-school meeting place and seen her set off for the nursery slopes committed to a rigorous session of stem turns. Then she had wandered away through the village again, looking at the shops and dawdling along to while away the time; finally she had arrived at the bottom of the chair-lift and spent some time watching the hardy ones start out on their expeditions up to Obergreutz. There was a queue as the ski-classes, jostling to keep together, waited impatiently for their turns. Liz saw Bernard amid his group take his seat and be borne aloft. She noticed no one exhibiting any form of dread as they boarded their chairs. If she were to enjoy the rest of this and any future ski-ing holiday she must somehow conquer her fear of this mode of transport. It had taken all her self-control to endure the ride up with her class the previous day. Twin chairs were not so bad; at least then you had a companion as you glided upwards among the trees, suspended by a fragile wire. But this chair-lift was a single-seater and you rode alone. The only good thing about it was that you were not required to wear your skis, for you disembarked at a station with a platform, not on a mountain slope off which you had at once to ski out of the way of the person travelling behind. Here, old Hans helped you to alight, clasping your skis, and you walked away.

She saw that today people were wrapping themselves in tarpaulins for protection against the weather. If she were to ride up, unhampered by the burden of her skis, with nothing to worry about except her actual person, perhaps next time she went carrying her skis she would manage better. Liz found ascending mountains far more of a problem than coming down. There was a restaurant at Obergreutz, above the chair-lift; she could fortify herself with a grog or two and then ride back again; the footpath down would be impassable after such a heavy snowfall.

She stepped into line.

Her turn came all too soon. She accepted a tarpaulin sheet from the attendant, wrapped it skirtwise round her hips, and went forward to the spot from which the chair would scoop her up. It came clanking round, she swung herself on it, seizing the pole by which it was suspended, and was whisked up and out, over the river and the roofs of the buildings below. She shut her eyes, groping for the bar to fasten herself in. Once that was safely closed in front of her she wriggled back, opened her eyes, and exhaled the breath she had held since take-off.

Fool, relax, she told herself. Small children travelled like this with neither qualms nor accident. She looked upwards, but the swirling snow blinded her and she could only just see the back of the person in the chair ahead. By no stretch of imagination could the scenery be admired in such conditions; survival was all.

The journey ended rather suddenly, for it was impossible to see the landing-stage from any great distance. Clumsily Liz unfastened the bar of her seat and got stiffly off on to the platform, shuffling in her tarpaulin skirt out of the way of the next alighting passenger. Everyone was going straight from the lift up into the restaurant above, which was brightly lit and very warm. Soon she was sipping a hot grog and beginning to thaw.

There was a constant bustle as people came and went; the intrepid ones would make the round trip several times in the morning. Liz could see through the window beside her some of these dedicated folk mounting higher still to take their turn on the twin anchor drag up which she had ridden herself yesterday in only light snow. She had gone up partnered by Jan van Hutter, a big, jolly Dutchman in her ski-class, whose height and weight had tilted the hook alarmingly.

Liz had just ordered her second grog when Francis Whittaker entered the restaurant. He pulled his black wool cap off as he came in and ran a hand over his greying hair, looking round the room to see who was there. Recognising Liz, he came over.

'Hullo! May I join you?' he asked, and sat down facing her. 'Depressing, isn't it, day after day? It's such damp snow, this stuff, gets in everywhere.' As he spoke he mopped his face with a large silk handkerchief; melted snow had trickled from his hair and eyebrows over his cheeks.

'It's not improving,' Liz said, peering through the window.

'No,' Francis agreed. 'It's getting worse,' he said. 'And it's so mild. They'll be closing the runs soon. Look, they're going to stop the anchor.'

Sure enough, higher up the slope people were being turned away from the double drag; it would be stopped when the last pair on it had reached the top.

'Are you going down alone?' Francis inquired.

'By chair. I'm a fraud, I'm not ski-ing,' Liz answered. 'I just came up for the ride and now I'm stoking up with some Dutch courage before risking my neck again.'

'Don't you like the chair? What on earth made you come up on a day like this, then?' Francis asked. 'You should have waited for the sunshine.'

'Then I might have waited till next year,' said Liz. 'I wanted familiarity to breed contempt.'

'And has it?'

'No. I doubt if it ever will.'

'It's perfectly safe.'

'Oh, I know that. But I don't like the disembodied feeling. I should understand absolutely if someone went berserk when travelling on it and flung themselves off.'

'What a gruesome idea,' said Francis.

'Why didn't Sue and I plump for somewhere where you go up the mountains by cable-car?' lamented Liz. From where she sat she could see the red cabin about to start down the valley to

Kramms. 'I suppose it would be rather a long way to walk to Greutz from Kramms if I went back by cable car.'

'You could get a taxi, perhaps. But the road might be blocked,' Francis said. 'What about flying? Do you hate that too?'

'No, oddly enough I don't. Inconsistent, isn't it? Of course, one's cocooned in a plane, it's not like being exposed to the elements, held back just by a metal bar one could easily slip under.'

'I suppose you could,' he conceded. 'I'm rather a snug fit myself in those chairs, once I'm fastened in. I enjoy them, I admit. It's always so peacefully quiet, and in fine weather it's glorious, with the mountains and the sky all around you and no human nearer than the chair in front.'

'If we had some good weather I might get braver,' Liz said. Her second grog came, and Francis ordered one for himself.

'A grog is a good idea, however one means to get down,' he remarked, watching while she stirred sugar into her steaming drink. 'This place must be doing well today; no one's going straight down.'

'Does it belong to the Scholler family? They seem to own most of Greutz.'

'No, it's run by people from Kramms,' Francis said.

'It must be a bit eerie, marooned up here when none of the lifts are running and it's snowing hard.'

'Horrible. I believe they go down to Kramms most nights, in fact, and only sleep up here if they do get stuck because of the weather.'

'I should think that must be quite often,' Liz observed grimly.

Various people spoke to Francis as they sat over their drinks, and she gathered that he had been to Greutz many times before. He talked to his various acquaintances in rapid German; Liz could not follow it at all.

'Sorry, how rude. You don't speak German?' he apologised.

'No. Only a few words for shopping,' Liz replied. 'You seem to be fluent.'

'I picked it up during the war,' Francis told her.

'You were in Germany?'

'I was a prisoner,' Francis said. 'But I managed to escape after a couple of years.'

'You must have had a few adventures!'

'I did. But I spent ages lying up, in hiding. That was frustrating more than anything.'

'In France?'

'No, in Austria. Quite near here,' he said. 'That was when I learned to ski.'

'You got into Switzerland eventually?'

'Yes, in the end.' Francis finished his drink. 'It was all a long time ago. Look, there's that fellow, what's-his-name, who sits at your table,' he added, looking over towards the doorway.

He seemed to want to change the subject. Liz would have liked to listen to an account of his war-time exploits, but she turned to see whom he meant, and recognised Bernard Walker coming into the restaurant at the tail of a group of men; he stood blinking behind his spectacles, which were all steamed up.

'Is he really with you?' Francis asked.

'No. We just travelled out together and were put at the same table for meals,' Liz said. 'Sue and I are on our own.'

'Oh, I see. It's sometimes difficult to make out the relationships within a group, when you're only on the fringe of it,' said Francis.

'It's sometimes difficult when you're right in the middle of it,' Liz remarked, and he laughed.

Alone of those who had travelled to Greutz under the auspices of Hickson's Holidays the previous weekend, and clearly at their own insistence, the Whittakers ate at a table apart; everyone else was placed at one big table.

'Bernard's an odd creature,' Liz went on. 'He's a real loner. He doesn't seem able to pause anywhere long enough to have a conversation.'

'He's certainly a glutton for punishment on the mountain,' Francis said. 'He seems to be with a class now, but I've noticed he goes up for an extra run at the end of every morning or afternoon, when everyone else is packing it in.'

'That's just the way to break a leg,' Liz said. 'Having another run when you're tired. It's a classic recipe for disaster.'

'What a pessimist you are,' said Francis. 'But you're right. That and running off the *piste* into deep snow.' He finished his drink and looked out of the window. 'We'd better be off,' he said. 'They'll stop the chair soon if it goes on snowing like this and then we'll have a problem.'

'Oh heavens!' Liz began pulling on her anorak, looking apprehensively out of the window. 'How horrible it looks. I must have been mad to come up.'

'You'll soon be safely back in beleagured, snowbound Greutz. Think of something nice while you're in your chair,' he advised.

'Like what?' asked Liz, with a smile. 'A Mozart concerto?'

'Well, I had in mind something less exalted, more on the lines of another hot grog,' Francis answered.

Liz thought of this encounter now as she walked down the village street. It had been a pleasant interlude in the dull day. What a pity Francis had brought his wife to Greutz, she reflected idly; many men left their non-ski-ing partners at home. A mild *affaire* would liven up the snowy siege they seemed to be in for, but the trouble was such things could seldom be kept within bounds, in her experience. It simply wasn't worth getting all steamed up over something that must finish in a fortnight; like Bernard, but for different reasons, she shrank from risk. It was Sue who always got involved, and now she was beginning to despair because no chance had come her way after a whole week in Greutz.

'Your charms are waning,' Liz had said dryly.

'There isn't any talent,' Sue had answered.

Liz sometimes wondered why they went on holiday together. They had been friends at college, and after Liz's marriage had crashed she had been glad of Sue, who was dependably kind and cheerful. But now she had carved for herself a settled life which did not expose her to emotional hazards. Only rarely did she admit her underlying loneliness. She disapproved when Sue became entangled; and Sue grew irritated at what she called Liz's 'stuffed shirt attitude'. But friendships formed in youth endure, despite the opposing views which may develop later.

If the snow went on falling like this it would be dreadful. There was nothing to do in a ski-resort but ski. Walking was limited to the few cleared paths in the village; you could not strike off up the mountain side. The Grand Hotel had a swimming pool, and that might occupy an hour, but some stimulating company would be quite a help. Apart from Francis Whittaker, whom Liz knew she would like to get to know, she had met no one remotely interesting. Penny, the courier, was merely a pleasant girl, intent on her own social life once the interests of her clients had been dealt with; Fiona, the disc jockey, was the sort of young woman Liz hoped never to find working in her office. Barbara Whittaker doubtless had the successfully married woman's contempt for her failed sister. Frau Hiller looked rather nice; she had a rich, warm laugh which Liz had heard once or twice. Liz knew she spoke some English, but had never had a chance to talk to her for unless she was with the Whittakers she seemed to spend most of her time in her room. The other people in the hotel were mostly German speaking, though whether they were in fact German, Austrian or Swiss Liz did not know, and they seemed to be in groups of four or six, all self-sufficient. Liz almost shared Sue's disappointment over Bernard and Sam, but she had met lone spinster men before and thought that this described the pair of them.

She managed to occupy half an hour by walking up and down the village street and going into all the shops. Then she decided to inspect the little church. She could make a circuit behind it, passing the few private chalets overlooking it, and returning by the pedestrian alley between the buildings. She turned off the main street and walked up the road that led to the church. The snow was deeper there, for fewer people went that way to keep the track clear. Wheel-marks showed that some traffic had passed, and a small Volkswagen drove by her, chains chinking as it went. The priest came out of the church as she approached; he wore a knitted cap like a skier, and his long grey beard flowed over the front of his brown cassock.

There was a faint smell of incense in the church; some candles burnt at a side altar, and there was a carved, brightly-painted Madonna and Child high above the chancel; otherwise it was surprisingly bare, with plain lime-washed walls. There was little to detain Liz; she inspected the few inscriptions, put some coins in the box as she left, and closed the door carefully behind her. The churchyard was covered in deep, smooth snow; what happened, she wondered, if anyone died and had to be buried? Digging a grave would be difficult.

She pushed such thoughts away and continued up the narrow lane. It was very quiet; no one else was wandering about this part of the village. Below, Liz could see a few figures disporting themselves on the nursery slopes where the two short drags were operating, but the chair-lift was idle; the mountain was silent and menacing, veiled in the heavy clouds that held the snow. The air was warm, and the wet snow stuck to her boots, like snow in England.

She came to the last chalet. Here the road petered out and became a footpath that wound back to the centre of the village, descending by steps cut in the side of the slope. The Volkswagen that had driven past her earlier was parked outside this final dwelling, and as Liz paused at the head of the path, a man came out of the chalet and opened the garage doors at the side of the house. Then he walked over to the car to put it away. He was tall and thick-set, wearing heavy-rimmed glasses, and his straight, dark hair was already powdered by a fine covering of snow.

Even through the falling snow Liz recognised him instantly.

'Patrick!' she cried, amazed.

He turned from the car to look towards her, and made out a small figure tightly encased in snow-proof garments, its anorak hood pulled close round the pale blob of its face, its eyes hidden behind yellow glasses, making identification impossible.

'What are you doing in Greutz?' continued Liz, and at these further words the mystery was solved.

'Liz! My dear old thing!' exclaimed Patrick Grant, and abandoning the car he embraced her fondly, planting a kiss on her lips, which tasted of snow. 'I didn't know you in your arctic kit,' he said. 'Come in, come in, and tell me all your news.'

'Hadn't you better finish what you were doing?' Liz asked him with some asperity.

'What? Oh, the car, you mean? It can wait,' said Patrick.

'You won't be able to move it soon,' she pointed out. 'Unless you want to use a shovel.'

'Oh, won't I? No, perhaps you're right.'

'Stop dithering, Patrick, and put it away. I won't vanish,' Liz said.

'I'm not so sure. You've done it before,' said Patrick. But he got into the car and drove it in to the garage, closing the doors upon it, while Liz waited on the porch. Then he returned to her, took her gloved hands in his and led her into the chalet.

'Surely it's term. Have you run away from Oxford?' Liz demanded.

'No. I was invited to give a paper in Innsbruck on Thursday, and Max Klocker asked me to spend the weekend here. This is his mountain retreat far from academic care,' Patrick told her. 'We've just been visiting a chum of his in Kramms; an interesting old man – used to be a concert pianist. We'd hoped to ski there, but the weather was too bad.'

He stamped his feet on the doorstep to shed the snow that clung to his boots, and helped Liz off with her anorak. While this was going on, a short, square man with a grey spade beard and brown eyes twinkling behind thick spectacles appeared in the hall.

'Another intrepid Briton, undeterred by our weather, eh Patrick?' he remarked.

'Mrs. Morris, Professor Klocker,' Patrick introduced them. 'Liz was up at Somerville when I was an undergraduate, Max.'

'Ah ha! You were students together?'

'Yes,' said Liz. 'For a time.'

For a time – until she had grown tired of waiting interminably on the river bank watching Patrick stroke his college eight. To teach him a lesson, she had started to go out with Geoffrey Morris, an economics graduate. Patrick had seemed unmoved by her defection; she had married Geoffrey and gone with him to Toronto. After five years of increasing discord they had parted; Geoffrey had gone to South America, which at least was far away. In due time they had divorced; Liz returned to England and worked as an editor in a publishing firm. There were no children. She had met Patrick again on a visit to Oxford. He had become a Fellow of St. Mark's College, and was later appointed Dean. From time to time now, they met; if Patrick was in London and had an hour or two to spare, he rang Liz up and took her out, treating her with the same casual affection he had displayed when they were undergraduates. After a few nostalgic regrets Liz had learned to adopt a similar brisk attitude to him; she had not seen him for months until today.

'Helga, Helga, we have a guest! Some tea!' the professor called, bustling away towards the kitchen regions of his chalet.

Liz took off her boots and stood them in the hall; better her feet in socks than pools of melted snow all over the professor's floor.

'You don't change,' Patrick told her with satisfaction, as he watched her.

'I haven't gone grey since our last meeting, if that's what you mean,' she said tartly. She had taken an afternoon off to go with him to a French film; after it, he had abandoned her in Oxford Street, hurrying back to Paddington for his train; there was a guest night at Mark's that evening which he did not propose to miss.

'Come along in, Mrs. Morris, come along,' the professor said, returning to them and directing them with shepherding gestures towards his study. 'No weather is too bad to daunt a British lady, I believe.'

'This very nearly is,' said Liz, who looked anything but daunted.

'Helga is bringing tea,' said Professor Klocker. 'With rum and lemon. You will like that.'

'It sounds wonderful.'

The professor's study was an attractive room. The timbered walls were lined with books; there were deep, leather-covered armchairs on either side of a log fire, a desk piled with papers, and more papers and books stacked about the floor.

'It's like your set at Mark's,' Liz said to Patrick.

'She means it's untidy, Max. Books all over the place,' grinned Patrick.

'I drive Helga to distraction with my ways,' the professor admitted, chuckling.

A plump woman bearing a tray laden with three steaming

glasses of tea now came in. She set her burden down, then produced from a pocket in her capacious skirt a pair of goatskin slippers for Liz. When she had departed, beaming, the professor took a bottle of rum from a cupboard by the hearth and poured large dollops from it into all their glasses.

'Helga will have been ungenerous,' he declared.

By the time Liz left the chalet it was too late to look for Sue at Ferdy's. Patrick walked with her back to the Gentiana. Inches of snow had fallen while she was in the chalet; their feet sank into the soft new covering.

'Come and have a drink,' Liz invited when they reached the hotel. 'Sue'll be upstairs. We've got a good stock of booze from the duty-free shop at Gatwick.'

So Patrick followed her up the creaking stairs, and waited in the passage while Liz opened the bedroom door to see if Sue was in a state to receive visitors.

'Look who's here,' she said, standing aside and beckoning Patrick to enter.

Sue, in the silver thread trouser suit with which she planned to dazzle the Gentiana that evening, was busy attaching her eyelashes.

'Patrick!' she shrieked. 'How wonderful! You can't be staying in Greutz too! Why didn't we know?'

'Make the most of him,' Liz recommended. 'He's due to leave tomorrow. But he's coming back here after dinner tonight, with a gorgeous bearded professor.'

When Patrick had gone, Sue gazed at Liz, marvelling.

'I can't think why you didn't marry him, instead of that rotten Geoffrey,' she said.

'Because he never asked me,' Liz replied. 'As you very well know. It never even occurred to him.'

## III

'The heavenly twins, oh dear,' murmured Sue when, late because of Patrick's visit, she and Liz joined Bernard and Sam for dinner at the table reserved for Hickson's clients. The four of them were alone, for Penny with her new contingent had not yet arrived; and there was no sign of Fiona, who often ate in the village with one or another of her constantly-changing admirers, dashing down to the discotheque just in time to prevent Frau Scholler setting forth irately from behind the reception desk to find out why the music had not started.

Sam looked up from his minestrone and made as if to rise; Bernard merely spooned up another mouthful and ignored them. Across the room at her solitary table Frau Hiller, who was reading *David Copperfield* in English, bowed at them and smiled. Francis and Barbara Whittaker had reached the chicken course; he raised a hand in greeting to Liz, who waved at him in return and was pleased to see Barbara frown at this innocent exchange.

Sue, as soon as she was seated, inspected the almost empty bottle of wine on the table.

'It's your turn, Bernard,' she said, without preamble. 'We need another bottle.'

It had been agreed at the beginning of the week that each in turn would order a bottle of the local wine to share around the table. Liz and Sue had already bought theirs, and this was the remains of Sam's second contribution. Bernard drank level with everyone else but so far had not subscribed at all.

He looked now at what was in his glass.

'Er – yes, it is my turn,' he admitted.

'You can order it, then, when Else brings our soup,' Sue told him firmly.

But when the waitress arrived with the two plates of soup Bernard would have let her go; Sue, however, detained her.

'Go on, Bernard,' she commanded, and he saw no help for it. He patted his thin, pale lips with his table-napkin.

'*Der wein, bitte*,' he said, indicating the bottle already on the table and carefully not looking at the pretty blonde girl with her round young breasts veiled only by a fine cotton blouse above the corseted bodice of her dirndl dress.

'*Bitte schon*,' Else replied, smiling.

Sue and Liz had discovered early in the week that Bernard

showed no desire to settle up for his share when anything was ordered for the group as a whole; this had happened at Ferdy's twice, where he had left them to pay for his coffee and cake saying he had to rush off. The first time they had let it pass, but after the second incident, scrupulous themselves about their debts, however small, they determined that he should not escape again.

After the bottle had arrived, and everyone had a full glass of wine, Liz took pity on Bernard, sitting with a sulky face eating fried chicken and beans.

'Are you going to the discotheque, Bernard?' she asked. It was most unlikely; sometimes he came in, looked anxiously around and left at once; he had never been seen to dance.

'I don't know. I've got to meet someone after dinner,' he replied. His voice was brusque.

'Who is she, Bernard?' Sue inquired.

Bernard did not answer. He munched on steadily, staring at his plate.

Sue raised her eyebrows and tried Sam. He was always more forthcoming if remarks were thrown at him, usually finding an answer even if he never started a conversation. He had been in the discotheque several times, though not dancing, but had seemed happy enough seated at a table watching the dancers.

'What about you?' Sue asked him.

'I'm joining the Whittakers. I expect we'll all come down,' he said.

'Oh good. We're meeting two chums of Liz's later,' Sue informed him. 'Two professors. We'll bring them along.'

'Patrick isn't a professor,' Liz protested.

'Well, he will be soon. One professor, then, and a don, since you're so fussy,' Sue said.

'And will they dance?' Sam inquired, sounding as if he thought it most unlikely.

'Of course. Most people enjoy dancing,' Sue said austerely. She had spent several evenings sitting beside Sam drinking beer and dropping hints, waiting in vain for him to lead her on to the floor.

Liz, when she suggested that Patrick and Professor Klocker

should come down to the Gentiana after dinner, had not pictured them in the nightclub, although the professor had seemed eager for Patrick to witness some of Greutz's night life.

'I'm sure the professor dances beautifully,' she said, imagining him waltzing. He would rotate in a stately style.

'Perhaps we might all join up, then, when your friends arrive?' Sam amazingly suggested.

"Oh, do let's. Good idea,' Sue agreed at once. Perhaps there was hope for Sam after all; the thaw might have begun.

When he had risen to join the Whittakers, and Bernard had silently left on his undisclosed mission, she said as much to Liz.

'Fool. He felt safe enough because he knows we've got two chaps lined up,' said Liz. 'He's scared to bits of us.'

'I can't think why,' Sue blandly said. Determined not to let Sam's mellowed mood be wasted she swept off to the cellar in his wake. Liz waited in the lounge for Patrick and Professor Klocker. She could hear the throb of the music from below, and when the two men appeared she explained, with a doubtful glance at the professor, that they were expected in the cellar.

'It's very noisy, as you can hear,' she warned.

'How about it, Max?' asked Patrick.

'It's most kind of your friends, Mrs. Morris,' said the professor. 'I have not visited this nightclub before. The Silvretta is nearer, when I have guests to entertain. I should like to see what the Gentiana has to offer, and I am sure Patrick cannot wait to waltz with you.'

Some men could still be gallant, anyhow, Liz thought dourly; she would not look at Patrick, who was masking his impatience with superlative ease. However, he might at least dance with Sue, which would cheer her evening.

She led the way down to the cellar, where the walls were papered in deep maroon with narrow gold stripes and the lighting was provided almost wholly by candles so that the effect was cavernous.

Sue, Sam and the Whittakers were seated at a long table as far away as it was possible to get from the actual discotheque. With them was Frau Hiller, looking rather bemused at the scene. Behind the turntables of her machine Fiona was enthroned, swaying to the music. She wore a purple cat-suit and her red hair was tied back in a huge purple bow. Her lips, too, were purple, and her face was white. She looked exhausted.

Liz introduced Professor Klocker and Patrick to the others, and for the first time since they had met a week before she saw Barbara Whittaker display some animation. Even at the bridge table she seemed languid. Now she patted the banquette seat, indicating that Patrick should sit beside her, and soon they were deep in conversation. Liz heard Patrick say: 'No, not medicine. English is my subject.'

Francis summoned the waiter. Barbara ordered brandy, but everyone else, including Frau Hiller, asked for beer.

'Is it still snowing, Professor Klocker?' Liz asked.

'Alas, yes. It is so unfortunate for everyone who wants to ski,' said the professor. 'And it is much warmer, too. That is a very bad sign.' His English was perfect, without a trace of accent. 'I doubt if Patrick will be able to leave tomorrow,' he added.

Liz's reaction to this was one of delight. Patrick's presence in Greutz would do a lot to brighten things up, although being marooned in the Alps in mid-term would hardly fit in with his plans.

'You are thinking the pass will be blocked?' Frau Hiller asked the professor.

'I should expect it to be closed already,' he replied. 'And if it continues to snow heavily there may be other troubles.'

'You mean avalanches? I heard a rumble in the distance yesterday,' Liz said.

'That was probably an artificial one. When a great quantity of snow falls in a short time and the temperature rises, the mass becomes insecure,' the professor said. 'Preventive measures are taken, and the snow is dislodged in small, harmless amounts by grenades, gunfire and so on. I have seen the ski instructors bring it down, too, knocking it with their poles, and roped to trees themselves in case they get swept away. But nature can still take powerful charge in the mountains. The road above Greutz is often blocked by falls, though it is usually cleared very quickly. However, don't be alarmed, Mrs. Morris. There hasn't been an avalanche in the village for very many years.'

'Oh, I'm not frightened,' Liz assured him. Patrick was now dancing with Barbara Whittaker; they were twisting in a dignified manner; she wished his pupils could observe him. 'I was just wondering whether the other people due from England today would get here. Penny Croft, the travel agent's representative, has gone to meet them in Zürich. What will happen if they can't get through?'

'They'll find rooms in the valley,' Professor Klocker said. 'The coach driver will telephone ahead to see if the road is clear, and if it isn't there will be a barrier at the foot of the mountain. We don't let travellers drive to the summit only to find the road closed on the other side.'

'You are accustomed to dealing with these trials in the mountains,' Frau Hiller said. Her English was slow and heavily accented, rather pedantic in style as if she had learned it from reading Victorian novels, but she seemed able to follow the quick speech of everyone else without trouble.

'We have to guard our reputation,' the professor said, twinkling at her. 'And we must keep our visitors not only content, but safe.'

'There will be plenty who won't be content if they can't ski,' said Liz ruefully.

'This weather is bad for the disposition,' the professor said gravely. 'The low barometric pressure is enervating. And it is disappointing to spend money on a holiday that should be sunny and exhilarating merely to stay indoors playing bridge. Is that how you have been occupying yourself, Mrs. Morris?'

'No. I don't play – at least I used to, but I've carefully unlearned it, it's so time-consuming,' said Liz. 'Once let it be known that you play and you're for ever being asked to make a fourth. But Frau Hiller plays, and the Whittakers, and Sam Irwin. They have a four all under one roof.'

'How convenient,' said the professor. 'It is at least an international game.' He moved his chair a little, the better to survey the floor. 'Very remarkable, is it not, this vogue for loud music? So unromantic.'

'It's primitive, like jungle drums, isn't it?' Liz agreed. 'No one seems to bother about being subtle any more.'

'What a pity,' said the professor. 'Tell me, that young woman clothed in purple, operating the music: is she really necessary?'

'Someone has to change the records, I suppose,' Liz answered. 'And she's decorative.'

'Who's decorative?' asked Patrick. He had finished his dance with Barbara and wanted to talk to someone else.

'Fiona, the disc-jockey,' Liz told him.

'Too emaciated,' he pronounced, after a scrutiny.

As she presided like a priestess over her modern altar, Fiona at this moment was surrounded by several acolytes, young men in tight pants and polo sweaters who talked to her, looked through the pile of records by her side, and at intervals draped themselves round her shoulders. She seemed unmoved by these demonstrations, but sometimes left her machine unattended while she danced with one of her admirers, or sat at a table drinking with another.

Patrick surveyed the room.

'Liz,' he said, 'there seems to be a friend of yours over by the door, trying to catch your eye. Somewhat of a giant.'

Liz peered through the smoky atmosphere and saw a large man with a round red face cheerfully waving at her.

'It's Jan van Hutter, from Rotterdam,' she said, waving back. 'He's in my ski-class.'

Jan was now approaching, weaving his way among the tables with huge strides. He had very bright blue eyes and wore a large smile.

'Elizabeth! My favourite lady!' he exclaimed, and kissed her hand.

'Do sit down,' said Patrick, making room for him. Liz saw the smirk on his face at the greeting Jan had given her and she kicked him hard under the table; her slippers were too soft to hurt his shins, unfortunately.

'Are you sure I do not intrude?' Jan asked, sitting down all the same.

'Of course not, Jan. I'm delighted to see you,' Liz said. 'Meet my friends. Sue you already know, I think.'

'Ah yes.' Jan beamed at Sue. 'We have met at Ferdy's, more than once.'

Liz continued with the introductions, leaving Patrick until last, to set him down if that were possible. He capped this act of hers by summoning the waiter and commanding further drinks.

'Elizabeth, you did not come to ski-school today,' Jan reproached her.

'No, Jan. I couldn't face another struggle in the blizzard,' she said. 'I took the day off.'

'You missed my triumph,' Jan told her solemnly. 'I had a wonderful morning. I have ridden to the top of the Schneiderhorn without falling from the drag-lift, and I have ski-ed down the White Run with only ten tumbles. But if you had not deserted me, Elizabeth, I would have done better still.'

'I do admire your dedication,' Liz said. Jan took so many bad falls each day that she constantly expected him to break one of his massive limbs, but all he ever did was laugh hugely, rise from the snow, shake himself like an enormous bear and lumber unsteadily off again.

'Elizabeth and I had an adventure on the drag-lift yesterday,' he told the company.

'We don't make a very good pair,' Liz said. 'Jan's so tall that he tilts the hook alarmingly.'

'That is true,' said Jan sadly. 'You need a partner of the same size. Riding with the small Elizabeth I was fixed on by only one boottock.' The Dutchman's excellent English contained some highly original examples of pronunciation.

Sue thought Liz had held the stage for long enough.

'Never mind, Jan,' she said. 'I'm making rapid progress on the nursery slopes and I'll ride with you when I'm in a higher class. There's more of me than there is of Liz.'

'Good, good,' said Jan, smiling. 'And will you dance with me now?'

Sue's feet had been tapping beneath the table to the rhythm of the music all the evening. She sprang up, delighted, at his invitation. They made a handsome couple on the floor.

'Come on, Liz,' said Patrick. 'You'll excuse us, Max.' He

took Liz by the hand and led her past the crowded tables, on to the dance floor.

'I like your professor,' Liz said. 'How did you meet?'

'We've corresponded for years,' said Patrick. 'He contributes to various journals I'm interested in. He's a great authority on Elizabethan drama – he spent some time in Cambridge as a young man just before the war. We met first at a seminar in Stockholm, two years ago.'

'What was your paper about?' Liz asked.

'Loosely speaking, guilt in Shakespeare's works, but I probed a bit,' said Patrick.

'I should think that's an inexhaustible subject,' said Liz. 'Lady Macbeth's insomnia, and so forth. And the ghosts.'

'Yes. Though they are often warnings, too,' said Patrick. 'Like Hamlet's father. Signs and portents are quite fun to think about.'

'You mean storms and things? Shipwrecks? Viola and Sebastian set adrift?'

'I wasn't thinking so much of the storms that trigger the plot as those which indicate the humour of the hour,' Patrick said. 'Like when Caesar was murdered, for example, and in *Lear*.'

'And in *Macbeth*, too.'

'Yes, but *Macbeth*'s a bit of a muddle,' Patrick said.

'I like it all the same,' said Liz.

'Oh, so do I. I like them all,' said Patrick. 'Each in its way.' He mused. 'Funny Irwin should be one of your little band.'

'And what's that supposed to mean? I don't see the connection.'

'Don't you remember his Mercutio? It was years ago. Perhaps it was when you were in Canada.'

'Do you mean he used to be an actor? He said he works in advertising.'

'So he does. Back view in commercial films, questioning housewives about their taste in soap flakes.'

'Don't tell me you watch television, Patrick!'

'I don't, much. But sometimes in other people's houses it's impossible to avoid. And I like to see my colleagues when they perform.'

'So that's why I thought I recognised Sam,' said Liz. 'I must have seen him on the box.' She watched plays and ancient movies when she was bored or lonely.

'I thought he'd go far,' Patrick said. 'He did this wonderful Mercutio, so deep, and an understated Shylock that was full of compassion.'

'Compassion in Shylock?'

' "If you prick us, do we not bleed?" ' Patrick quoted. 'And that business of Jessica and the ring.'

'It was the ring he was so keen to get back, not so much his daughter.'

' "It was my turquoise: I had it of Leah when I was a bachelor: I would not have given it for a wilderness of monkeys," ' repeated Patrick.

'Well, compassion or not, why did Sam leave the stage?' Liz asked.

'I don't remember the details – trouble over a contract or something. He fell from grace, and from the public eye.'

'So now he just does telly-ads?'

'Maybe he gets bit parts in films. I wouldn't know.'

'What a sad story,' said Liz. 'I'll be nicer to him now I know it. He seems quite harmless, but vague and remote, and he's got such an expressionless face, you feel there's no one there behind it, talking to you. He's quite friendly with the Whittakers; they're remote, too, or she is. I don't think she likes being on a package tour and having a hob-nob with riff-raff like us. Producing you and the professor will have done our status good with her.'

'Much you care,' grinned Patrick. 'What about her husband?'

'Francis? Oh, he's nice,' said Liz airily. 'Not snooty at all. I think he'd like to mix a bit. Still, he does escape all day; she doesn't ski and he's rather good.'

'Odd they chose this sort of holiday,' Patrick remarked.

'He says she likes sitting in the sun and playing bridge.'

'Oh, you've had a confidential chat, then?'

Liz glared at Patrick.

'We had a grog together, up at Obergreutz, quite by chance,' she told him frostily. 'Francis learned to ski during the war. He was a prisoner but he escaped.'

'Hm, did he, indeed? How interesting,' Patrick said. 'What's his job?'

'I don't know. Let's guess and have a bet.'

'Right. Loser buys two tickets for the Old Vic, play of her choice,' said Patrick.

'Play of his choice,' Liz corrected. 'I guess, hmmm, let me see. Maybe a profession. He's not a doctor, nor a schoolmaster or he wouldn't be away now; could be a solicitor but I don't somehow think so. Seems to be comfortably off, her clothes are all expensive. Management consultant?'

'That's your final word?'

'Yes, why not?'

'You aren't very observant,' Patrick said. 'Haven't you noticed the healthy patina to his complexion? It isn't just the holiday, it's much more basic. He works out of doors. His hands are calloused. He's away from home in winter, when farmers can take leave. But I don't think he's an ordinary farmer. Not arable, livestock or poultry, anyway.' He meditated. 'Landscape gardener,' he decided.

'Dutch treat if we're both wrong?' said Liz, quickly, her own confidence shaken by Patrick's deductions.

'Naturally. Dinner on me in either case,' said Patrick graciously, smiling at her.

The record stopped. Fiona shouted something indistinguishable into the microphone and a tuneless beat blared forth from the speakers.

'Goodness, what primordial stuff,' said Patrick.

'It's meant to be like heart-beats. Back to the womb and all that,' Liz informed him. 'Does it turn you on?'

'No, too crude. I prefer to smooch to subtle melodies,' said Patrick, clasping her closely.

Liz was quite willing to smooch with Patrick, but it was impossible to do so in harmony with this so-called tune, and they gave up. Soon afterwards Frau Hiller said it was her bedtime and she left the party; the professor said it was time for him and Patrick to go home. Liz went up to the hall to see them off, promising to return to the nightclub when they had gone.

At the reception desk, conferring in rapid German with Frau Scholler, was Penny Croft, in her bright green uniform cloak and cap. She saw Liz and waved a hand, not interrupting her flow of speech.

'Who's the fugitive from Sherwood Forest?' inquired Patrick as he put on his coat.

Liz told him.

'Conditions can't be as bad as we thought, since they've managed to get here,' she said. 'I've been thinking we've been having a bit of Shakespeare's ominous weather these past days.'

The hotel porter came through the swing doors as she spoke, carrying a suitcase in either hand and with two more slung on a strap across his shoulders. He was covered in snow. Bernard Walker followed him into the hall, almost fell over Penny and said, '*Entschuldigen Sie, bitte,*' then added, 'Oh, it's you, Penny, sorry.' He stamped his feet on the matting and vanished into the men's cloakroom, near where Liz, the professor, and Patrick were standing.

Penny had finished her monologue to Frau Scholler.

'We made it, you see,' she said to Liz. 'But we had to walk up the lane, the bus got stuck down at the bottom. I was just telling Frau Scholler all about it.'

'Did you have an awful journey?'

'It might have been much worse. There's only one line of traffic over the pass, and it won't be open much longer at this rate.'

Liz turned to Patrick.

'You'll be marooned here after all,' she said. She introduced him and the professor to Penny, and explained that Patrick was supposed to fly back to England the next day.

'There's no sign of the snow slackening,' Penny said. 'And it's much too warm. You've had it, Dr. Grant.'

'Never mind,' said Patrick calmly. 'If Max can bear with me, I can certainly endure being stuck here for a day or two. Innsbruck will have to manage without him, and Mark's will grind on in my absence, I've no doubt. I'll be in touch, Liz, if the pass is closed tomorrow.' He kissed her lightly, and then he and the professor, who had a torch, went through the swing doors into the swirling snow, where their two figures and the pale light of the torch were soon swallowed up by the masking blanket of the blizzard.

'Have you parked all your people?' Liz asked Penny.

'Yes. The ones at the Silvretta all know each other; they're quite a cheery lot, young, and keen to ski. We've got two couples here, the Fosters and the Derringtons.'

'Shall we like them?' Liz inquired, and as Penny hesitated she laughed. 'Come on, don't be so discreet, what are your first impressions? It looks as if we'll all be cooped up together while the blizzard lasts; let's be warned.'

'Well, let me see.' Penny was still cautious. Finally she admitted: 'Roy Foster did a good deal of ear-bashing in the bus. He seems to have ski-ed all over the Alps. His wife's a quiet little thing; she was a bit upset by the flight, I think. Evidently it was rather bumpy. Frankly I was surprised they managed to keep the airport open. The Derringtons are professional travellers, the kind that can be useful on a tour because they know all the answers and help with the sheep, but they can be a bit too bossy sometimes, those types.'

'You mean they organise outings and so on?' Liz shuddered.

'Mm. That sort of thing. She's not English, she's got quite a strong accent. They both speak German very well and they had all the right kinds of money wherever we stopped and shepherded everyone in for supper and ordered drinks and things. It was quite restful for me, really.'

'You don't sound very convincing!' Liz said. She was amused by this enlightening little outburst from the hitherto imperturbable courier.

'Well, they were helpful, but it'll be a bit exhausting if they expect me to be as tough and efficient as they are,' said Penny disarmingly.

'They sound rather formidable.'

'Don't be put off. It's probably just me making a wrong snap judgement,' said Penny. 'But in this job you get so that you slot people into different categories pretty quickly. Roy Foster's the kind that complains at the least thing, and expects five-star luxury on a package-deal. The Derringtons won't expect exotic food or anything like that, but they'll set impossible physical standards. Maybe Bernard will pal up with them and take his masochistic self ski-ing in their company.'

'You think he's a masochist?'

'Well, don't you? He's always punishing himself with great endurance tests, and he never looks as if he's the slightest bit happy. Fiona and I call him the Lone Ranger, but that business of being a wolf on the prowl is all an act. He hasn't moved from first base.'

Liz laughed.

'I never knew you were such a psychologist, Penny,' she said. 'Heaven defend me from your perceptive eye. Come on down and have a drink if you aren't too tired. Everyone's in the nightclub, and look, even your would-be wolf is on the way to join us.'

As they talked, Bernard had emerged from the cloakroom, still in his navy-blue anorak, from the pocket of which protruded his woolly cap. He hesitated in the hall, then took off his anorak, opened a zip pocket in it and removed his wallet, and hung the jacket among the others on the long rack on the wall. He wore a black-and-white patterned Norwegian-knit sweater which hung loosely on his narrow frame. He slid the wallet into a pocket in the shirt he wore beneath the sweater. It gave him an odd appearance.

'Big deal,' said Penny. 'That's all I need.' She grinned. 'But I could use a drink, thanks. I told my people I'd be down there for a while if they wanted a quick one before bed, but I should think they're all pretty whacked. Even the Derringtons admitted the flight was rough. They circled round at Zürich, wafting up and down in the gusts, several times before they could come down. Not nice at all.'

'You can sleep tomorrow,' Liz said.

'I doubt it. That Silvretta crowd are raring to go. Whatever the day's like they mean to get set with skis and ski-school tickets and what-not right away.'

Penny's job was certainly demanding. She had to be cheerful and available, know all the answers, and cope with every emergency. It was a myth to think that things did not get disrupted in countries which every year had a considerable snowfall.

The others were still enjoying themselves in the cellar. Fiona had abandoned her machine, which was playing a Tyrolean waltz, and was sitting beside Jan on the bench by the wall. Barbara and Sam were dancing, and Francis and Sue were talking. Bernard was nowhere to be seen. When Liz and Penny joined the group Francis ordered another round of drinks.

'We owe someone for two beers already,' said Liz.

'Patrick paid for one,' said Sue. She looked dreamy, and kept glancing at Jan, who had greeted his new beer with what seemed to be an unabated thirst. Liz sighed. She knew that look.

'Oh, did he?' she said aloud. 'Well, he can afford it. You did the other one, didn't you, Francis. I'll square up now, I've got our purse.' She and Sue kept a special purse into which they paid equal sums as required which were used for joint expenses.

'Stop fretting about your independence and come and dance while there's a decent tune playing,' Francis said, standing up.

Liz meekly pocketed the purse and went with him to the small space of floor left clear for dancing. The music was the theme from *Un Homme et Une Femme*, which she could never hear unmoved; the curious, haunting melody had its usual effect upon her now, and she was at once aware of the feel of Francis's thick wool sweater under her hand as it rested on his shoulder, and the touch of his palm, calloused as Patrick had observed. Or was it really just the music?

'Relax. This is for fun. I don't bite,' he said into her ear, gathering her to him. 'Nice little tune, isn't it? Let's enjoy ourselves.'

Liz hoped Barbara would not look their way, and then, contrariwise, hoped she would. Why? Nothing was at risk. She kept away from other people's husbands, in fact she kept away from everyone. So she could enjoy the moment safely enough; nothing could hurt her, here in the Gentiana. They moved closer together.

'That's better,' he said. He hummed the tune softly under his breath for a while, and then asked her, 'What happened to your husband.'

'We just couldn't get along.'

'One of those mutually destructive set-ups, was it? It happens all the time.'

'Mm. I know. Frightening, isn't it? Can one ever succeed?'

'Sometimes it's possible to fight through to a state of neutral tolerance,' he said.

'Isn't that very hypocritical?'

'It depends on what's at stake. There can be complications, material things that bind.'

Had he married a rich wife to whose tune he must now dance? Or were there children? He hadn't mentioned them, but that must be the answer, if he were speaking personally, and she thought he was.

'Sometimes crumbs of pleasure come one's way,' he went on, holding her more closely. Liz did not want to be a crumb for anyone, but she was powerless to draw back from him. 'You, on the other hand, would always choose to run away,' Francis said. 'You miss a lot.'

Most appropriately, the music now switched to *Strangers in the Night*, perennially a favourite in ski-resorts no doubt because it was so apt, and they both began to laugh. Maybe there was something to be said for his philosophy, Liz thought, but she feared any search for crumbs on her part would leave scars. Even Sue, so much simpler in her outlook, mourned briefly every time.

When the music ended they went back to the table and found Bernard there; he was sitting uneasily perched on the banquette as though preparing for rapid flight. Fiona left her place and wove a crooked course across the floor to her machine; she put on a stack of records and then zigzagged back.

'That'll keep it going for a time,' she said. She drew herself up, slight in her purple outfit, the striking red hair now escaping from its knot and falling over one shoulder. Languidly she gazed round the room, shrugged, and then flopped on to the bench beside Sam, draping herself over him. He frowned, unwrapped her arms from round his neck and pushed her towards Bernard, who shuddered.

'Oh God, Fiona,' said Penny in a despairing voice. 'You've been mixing them again.'

'I'm all right. Don't be such a stick,' said Fiona. 'Relax, enjoy yourself.'

'If the Schollers see her in this state there'll be trouble,' Penny muttered. 'She's done it once too often as it is.' She sprang up. 'I'll get the waiter to bring some black coffee.'

It seemed as if more than black coffee would be needed. Fiona was now tweaking Bernard's ear and mumbling into it. Bernard looked as if he feared imminent rape.

'Do stop it, Fiona, there's a good girl,' he besought her, trying to wriggle out of range. He could not move far, or she would topple over.

'Don't be shy,' Fiona crooned to him. 'I think you're a dark horse really.' She twined one of his mouse-coloured curls round her fingers, then, with unsteady hands, removed his glasses. Liz stretched across the table to take them from her wavering grasp and laid them down in safety. All were fascinated by this assault on Bernard and no attempt to rescue him was made. Barbara, after a moment, decided to avert her eyes from the distressing scene and began to ask Jan about his home in Rotterdam, where his wife was at this moment expecting the arrival of the fourth little van Hutter. The others watched while Bernard's face turned from a weathered pallor to a suffused crimson.

Fortunately for him, the coffee soon came.

'Make her drink it, for heaven's sake,' said Penny. 'Oh, here are my people.' She pushed the cup across to Fiona and stood up, putting on a pleased smile as two men and two women came towards the table.

'Hullo, there,' she greeted the arrivals. 'So you decided to come down. Fine!' She started her introductions at the end of the table furthest from Fiona's sad exhibition, but in the end it had to be noticed. Fiona gazed dimly at the newcomers, then began to mutter into Bernard's sweater. He, by this time, had an arm round her, but only in order to stop her from falling into his lap.

Freddie Derrington was a big man with curling dark hair and sideburns and a large moustache. He was about fifty. His wife, Hilda, was also dark, sturdily built, and much the same age. The Fosters, Roy and June, were young.

'These two are on their honeymoon. They got hitched yesterday,' Freddie revealed when the introductions were complete. 'That calls for champagne, don't you agree? Waiter!'

Fiona sat up, pushing Bernard away.

'Champagne, did I hear?' she asked. 'Goody.'

By the time the party broke up it was after half-past twelve. Sue did not come upstairs until some time after Liz; while she embarked on her nightly ritual of creaming and massage, Liz lay staring up at the bedroom ceiling thinking about the evening.

'Poor honeymooners,' she said at last. 'What a start.'

'They've probably been sleeping together for months. There's nothing much to start, is there?' Sue said.

'Who's the cynic now?' Liz answered. 'Pity everyone had to know it's their honeymoon.'

'Why? Times have changed since you were a blushing bride.'

'Yes, and not always for the better.'

'What's got into you tonight?' demanded Sue. 'You're not usually sentimental.'

There was no reply. Liz, in her mind's eye, still saw June Foster's white, alarmed face as she watched her husband steadily get drunk, both of them silent, while the Derringtons described in vivid detail the flight out, the adventures of the coach drive from Zürich, and their hopes for the morrow's ski-ing. Fiona had glued herself to Bernard once again, limpet-like, and he, penned in on the other side by the bulk of Freddie Derrington, seemed too bemused to seek escape.

Sue got into bed at last and pulled the *duvet* round her shoulders; for a few minutes there were rustles, squeaks and sighs as she made herself ready for slumber. Liz lay silently through all this, and soon her even breathing indicated that Sue slept. But Liz was wakeful. The events of the day ran through her mind like the unreeling of a film.

She recalled her meeting with Francis in the restaurant at Obergreutz; their conversation had been only superficial, but there was something about him that made her thoughts keep coming back to him. She had been happy when he suggested they should dance; all evening she had hoped he would. Beware! Danger! she told herself, and switched her thoughts to the safer subject of Patrick. How strange that he should be in Greutz. What a pity he had left the nightclub before the new arrivals came; he would enjoy theorising about them. Patrick always speculated about everyone he met and declared no one was wholly uninteresting; he had an uncanny way of spotting things that no one else would notice. By that token, it was lucky he hadn't seen her dance with Francis. The evening had been full of changing moods. Fiona had been funny, making a set at Bernard; she was too drunk to remember who he was by the end. He seemed to forfeit everyone's sympathy; no one appeared to care at all about his discomfiture. And outside the snow had gone on falling, endlessly, as if the sky would never clear again.

She had almost drifted into sleep when a board creaked on the landing outside. Wide awake at once, she waited, but the noise was not repeated. Had Sue locked the door? It was unlikely that a prowler would come in, but one never could be sure. Liz got up and tried the handle. It opened, and she looked outside. At the far end of the dimly-lit corridor she could see a large male figure moving silently away. She thought it looked like Freddie Derrington, but it could have been Jan, hopeful of finding a complaisant Sue available.

Liz withdrew softly, closed the door and locked it, and got into bed.

# PART THREE

# Sunday

## I

ALL THAT night the snow fell heavily, and by morning no sharp edges remained anywhere, only gentle contours where the snow ploughs had cut sheer ridges earlier by the roadside. The roofs of buildings bore thick helmets, sparkling crystalline and in places fringed with gleaming icicles where warmth from within had melted some of the snow.

At breakfast, there were no rolls; instead, slices of drab grey bread filled the baskets on the tables. Not only was the mountain pass closed, but also the road along the valley to Kramms, where the bakery was.

'Oh dear,' said Sue, who looked forward greedily to her crisp rolls each morning. 'Well, I suppose it can't be helped. There's honey, though, I see.' She reached across Sam and took a foil-wrapped portion of honey out of the dish.

'Sorry,' he mumbled, pushing the butter towards her. 'I'm still half asleep. It was rather noisy in the annexe last night.'

'I should think it might have been,' said Liz. 'I'm surprised Fiona made it back there – she did I suppose?'

'Oh, ultimately,' Sam replied, and said no more.

Penny came rushing in, looking fresh and rested, her fair hair held back from her face by a wide green band which matched her sweater. She carried a sheaf of papers and said she was in a great hurry.

'That crowd at the Silvretta's been on the phone already,' she said. 'I'm meeting them in ten minutes at Winkler's to get skis.

The Derringtons have got their own, and I shouldn't think the Fosters will want to bother today, but send them along if they do.'

'Surely there won't be any ski-ing? It's snowing just as hard as ever,' Liz said.

'Oh, I think there will. It is a little colder than it was, and Frau Scholler says the *lehrers* have gone up. I heard the snowcat when I came across. Anyway, I must get all these keen people fixed up so that they're ready for anything.'

She drank two cups of coffee straight off and ate a slice of bread. Just as she was about to leave the Derringtons appeared.

'The lifts are functioning. We'll be up the Schneiderhorn by half-past ten,' said Freddie briskly. He looked very workman-like this morning in his white cotton polo shirt and tight black ski-pants. Hilda was identically dressed; she had seemed sturdy enough the evening before, but now she was revealed as really muscular, with broad, powerful shoulders and strong, thick legs.

Liz looked at Freddie's hands as he tackled his breakfast in a hearty manner. They were tanned and bore scars on the square, capable fingers. Another manual worker, she decided.

'Have you got over your adventures in the night?' Penny asked them.

'Yes,' said Hilda. 'Something like this always happens to me. It makes me very annoyed.'

'What adventure did you have?' asked Sue.

'I got locked into the bathroom,' said Hilda. Penny was right about her accent, Liz thought. It was slight, but definite, and she said 'this' where the use of 'that' would have been more Anglo-Saxon. It was not French : the intonation was more central European. 'I was a prisoner for half-an-hour,' she continued. 'How did you hear about it?'

'Frau Scholler told me this morning. She couldn't understand it,' Penny said.

'Someone playing games, I think,' said Hilda.

It seemed that the Derringtons had their own bathroom, but it was in the old part of the building and was approached from the landing, not their bedroom, so that it needed locking. The key had to be used on the outside when the room was not in use, to prevent invasion by other guests, and inside when it was occupied. Because the hour was so late, Hilda had not troubled to lock herself in, leaving the key on the outside of the door. It had been turned on her, and then removed.

'What an extraordinary thing to happen,' said Liz. She thought of the figure she had seen on the landing in the night.

'Some prankster, I suppose,' said Hilda.

'I didn't hear you screaming and battering down the door,' remarked Sue. 'I suppose your husband wondered where you were, and found you.'

'Yes, he did, at last,' said Hilda. 'It was a very childish trick, whoever played it, and now the key is lost.' From the look she gave Freddie it was obvious whom she suspected: but why lose the key? Liz decided some people looked for kicks in the strangest places, and changed the subject, asking Hilda where they lived in England. In Kent, was the answer, near Maidstone.

Liz did not know Kent, apart from Dover docks, so that was conversationally a dead end, but she persevered and discovered that the Derringtons had a mink farm.

'We pelt them in November. After that we have a rest. As long as we're home in March, for the mating, we can leave them in the winter,' Hilda explained.

This was a good one. Patrick would never think of it.

'How many mink have you got?' she asked.

'Fifty males and a hundred females,' answered Freddie.

'Is that a lot?'

'Pretty fair, if we get good results with the kitts. We do it all ourselves, with the help of one man and an occasional pupil, so we cut our overheads on wages and so forth.'

'Aren't they rather nasty little things?' Sue inquired. 'Like rats?'

'They bite you if you give them half a chance,' said Hilda. 'If they get their teeth in your flesh they won't let go. You have to force open their jaws.'

That accounted for the scars.

'I suppose you've got a fabulous coat?' Sue said.

Hilda laughed somewhat bitterly.

'Not yet,' she said. 'Mine's made of nylon fur. We have to sell all our pelts.'

Both the Derringtons ate a substantial breakfast, with boiled eggs to supplement the bread and honey. Hilda's concentration as she scraped every vestige from the empty shell reminded Liz of Bernard, who always enjoyed his food : he was not yet down. The Fosters arrived just as Penny, who had been side-tracked from her plan of hurrying to the sports shop by the Derringtons, was about to leave at last. Everyone hid their surprise at seeing these two so early, and Penny asked them if they wanted skis at once.

'Oh yes,' said Roy. 'June must get going straight away. She's never ski-ed before, she can't waste any time.' He was a stocky young man with rather long hair that curled over his collar, and a red face. June was pale, plump, and pretty in a subdued way; she had large blue eyes and a gentle expression.

'You've done a lot of ski-ing. You told us yesterday,' Penny said.

'Oh yes,' said Roy. 'I come out every year.'

'You're all very good, I expect,' said June, addressing the whole table, her gaze moving round from face to face.

'We're not,' said Sue robustly. 'I'm the dunce, June. You'll soon catch me up. Once you can stop you'll feel wonderful.'

'I'm not expecting to be able to start, let alone stop,' June said. I'm sure it must be fun,' she added, but she looked extremely doubtful.

'Of course it is. You'll soon get the hang of it, a fit girl like you,' said Roy. He told the others, 'June's a good horsewoman; she's pretty fit.'

Penny said she would meet them at the Sportshop Winkler, and when she had gone Francis Whittaker came over to the table; Barbara went straight out of the dining-room.

'Who's ski-ing this morning?' Francis asked. 'Are you, Liz?'

'I don't know.' Liz looked through the window at the grey vista. 'It doesn't look at all inviting.'

'I rather doubt if the Schneiderhorn drag will be working, but why don't you do the White Run? I'll come with you. I'm sure you don't want to go to ski-school, you'll get frozen hanging about while everyone does their party-piece.'

Liz looked at him.

'I'd drive you mad by going too slowly,' she said.

Francis laughed.

'I don't go mad so easily,' he said. 'I shan't be in any hurry.'

'I don't like the idea of ski-ing alone,' Liz admitted.

'Very proper,' said Freddie, his mouth full of egg.

'Well, it's all right as long as someone knows where you've gone and will notice if you don't turn up again,' said Francis. 'You'll come, then, Liz?'

Why not? Hadn't he said she always ran away? This time she wouldn't.

'All right,' she said. They arranged to meet at the foot of the chair-lift at ten-fifteen, after the first rush was over.

Later, in the bedroom, Sue looked at her.

'You fancy him, don't you?' she said.

'Who? Francis? Don't be silly.'

'Watch it, girl, I'm telling you, even if you don't know it yourself. I'm never wrong,' Sue stated.

'You've got a novelette mind,' Liz said curtly. She folded her frilly nylon nightdress and laid it neatly on her pillow, ready for the maid when she came to do the room. 'Don't judge my reactions by your own.'

'Methinks you do protest too much,' Sue said blithely. 'But one can't get up to much mischief here, I suppose, more's the pity. Everyone would know about it in five minutes.'

It was as well she realised that, Liz thought grimly, remembering how Sue and Jan had held hands under the table in the nightclub the evening before.

'I wonder how Fiona is today,' she said. 'She must have a mammoth hangover.'

'She looked about forty last night, didn't she, ginned up to the eye-balls,' Sue said. 'I suppose she's only about twenty-four really.'

'If as much,' said Liz. 'Well, are you going to go to ski-school? If you are, I'll walk down with you.'

'You'll be too early for your date. Don't be so eager,' Sue said.

'I want to buy some postcards,' Liz answered coldly. Sue could be very trying.

'O.K. Come on then,' Sue agreed.

They put on their heavy boots, zipped up their anoraks, made sure they had money, goggles and gloves, and clumped downstairs. There were two entrances to the ski-room; a swing door from the hall led down some stairs and into it at one end, and there was an outer door from the lane. They took the latter, leaving the hotel by the main entrance and pausing outside to look at the barometer on the wall. It was colder, but the pressure remained very low. Though it was still snowing the flakes were much smaller and less dense, and it was possible to see more of the village than had been visible for days. The chair-lift, with only a few passengers, was working steadily.

The ski-room was deserted. It was lit only by one electric bulb, and as it was an L-shaped, narrow apartment it was quite difficult to find the right skis in the gloom. Racks ran along the walls on both sides, and by the number of skis still stacked there it was clear that few of the Gentiana's visitors were braving the day. Some toboggans were untidily stowed at one end of the room, and pools of water from melting snow gathered on the floor.

They walked down the hill together. A new track had been cleared in the snow and it was easy to see what a huge amount had fallen in the night: almost a foot. At the wooden bridge they parted. Sue crossed over to the ski-school assembly point, where there was only a meagre attendance so far, no doubt partly due to the weather, but Sundays were always slack owing to the change-over of visitors. Most weekends, skiers came up to Greutz from towns in the valley; they crowded the lifts and runs, and filled the hotel bars. None would get in today, with the roads blocked. Liz stood by the river bank and watched Sue stride over to join her group; she was easy to pick out in her rust-coloured outfit. A huge man detached himself from a waiting cluster of people, all standing with skis stuck into the deep snow beside them, and greeted her with a hug; it was Jan. Liz turned back to the village and went into the newsagent's. She spent some minutes choosing several postcards, but at this rate she would be back in England herself before they could arrive, since there was no transport out of Greutz. Emerging from the shop, she saw both the

Whittakers and Frau Hiller entering the Silvretta hotel on the other side of the street.

Liz had left her skis propped against the wall of the shop. She picked them up and hoisted them over her shoulder, balancing them so that she needed only a touch to keep them in position with her left hand, and began to walk slowly down to the chair-lift terminus. Francis was presumably escorting his wife and Frau Hiller to a bridge appointment; he would catch her up.

Before he did so the Derringtons overtook her, striding briskly, each carrying a smart pair of Head skis and looking very professional in their all-black outfits complete with goggles. They were not talking, and they did not recognise Liz.

Francis carried her skis up on the chair for her.

'This is for fun, remember,' he said. 'Would you like me to come behind and pick up the bits, or shall I lead the way?'

'You go first, please,' she said. She would have to follow, then, and perhaps the sight of his broad back ahead would give her courage.

When they had both been swept over the wide, dark cleft of the river he turned to wave to her. Greatly daring, she waved back. It was still snowing, but with fine cold flakes, not huge blobs like those that had fallen through the night. In places the snow had blown in drifts close to the chair, so that there was no great distance in the drop. But if you fell, what depths you would be buried under, Liz imagined with a shudder. In some places the *piste* wound between the supporting pylons and passed below; the skiers coming down were quiet, not shouting to each other as they might have done in sunny weather.

Up on the Schneiderhorn, Professor Klocker and Dr. Patrick Grant were also out ski-ing that morning. Patrick wore borrowed boots and skis from an array the professor kept in the cellar of his chalet for visitors. They went down the White Run for their first descent, so that Patrick could get the feel of the skis before tackling something harder, and the professor could assess his ability. Professor Klocker led the way, a neat, compact figure in his dark outfit, turning and swaying with economical movements.

'You are good, Patrick. You have done a lot of ski-ing, I see,' he pronounced as they unclipped their skis at the bottom of the run, ready to take the chair up again. 'What a pity the weather is so bad. One can do so many expeditions from the top of the Schneiderhorn; there is a big network of lifts that link up with it. It is too bad to risk going down to Kramms and back by cable car.'

It was obvious that his host enjoyed ski-ing, which was a relief to Patrick, who did not want to feel the outing had been undertaken merely for his entertainment.

'Are you very annoyed at not being able to get back to Innsbruck?' Patrick asked.

'No.' The professor shook his head. 'I have a lecture on Wednesday, and it will be a pity if my pupils are deprived of it, but at the moment I am more concerned with finishing my book than with my teaching. Lamentable, is it not?' He looked at Patrick quizzically. 'I do much less teaching nowadays, and more research.'

When they reached Obergreutz for the second time they found that the anchor drag lift was operating, and they rode on up to the summit. With the snow coming down gently and the thick cloud on the mountain, it was like being in dense fog. Patrick knew that in Oxford on a day like this he would do everything possible to avoid having to put his nose outside the comfort of St. Mark's, yet here he was, happy enough to follow the professor's lead.

'What a pity you can see nothing,' cried Max, waving a ski stick around as they rode up side by side, skis cutting smooth parallel tracks in the soft new snow. 'In good weather the mountains of three countries are visible from the top.'

'I didn't realise Italy was so near,' said Patrick.

'It's closer than Switzerland by the direct route,' Max answered.

'Can you ski across?'

'No. The north face of the mountain is too steep to climb. But in summer rich tourists come up by helicopter to ski on the glacier. I prefer to walk, myself, in that season.'

Patrick was sorry to miss the panorama of the mountain peaks. As things were, it was not too easy to keep the professor's back in sight as they ski-ed down, for he set a brisk pace. It would be a simple matter to lose one's way in this weather; few people had come up to the top and there were not so very many tracks to follow. Patrick had not done much ski-ing in deep snow, and he felt quite pleased with himself when he regained the beaten *piste* without misadventure.

'We'll take the Red Run this time, Patrick,' Max said, as they curved round the shoulder at Obergreutz below the restaurant. Here the cloud was much less thick, and they could see groups of skiers making their way down. He started off, and Patrick followed. Where the runs divided the professor waited for Patrick to catch him up; he stood resting, leaning on his sticks, looking down the mountain. Patrick, over-confident, missed a turn and fell; the soft snow found its way up his sleeves and down his neck as he got to his feet again.

'There has been an accident, I think,' the professor said, pointing below, when Patrick joined him.

Patrick looked in the direction he indicated, and saw a knot of people gathered round someone on the ground.

'Oh dear. Shouldn't we go down and help?'

'There seem to be plenty of people on the spot already, and since our subject is literature, not medicine, we might not be much use,' said Max. He looked back up the mountain. 'There must be a stretcher at Obergreutz. We'll wait a few moments to make sure it goes down – that is, if it's needed. Perhaps the victim is merely winded and will soon be on his feet.'

They were still standing there, watching, a few minutes later when Francis Whittaker and Liz reached them, going down the White Run for the second time. Liz had her goggles pushed up over her forehead, and her cheeks were flushed with exhilaration. She recognised Patrick and the professor just before she drew level with them, and stopped with a flourish that drew praise from Patrick.

'What are you staring at?' she asked, and then saw the group of people clustered below. 'Someone's hurt?'

'Must be. Here's the blood-wagon,' said Francis, and past them, travelling fast, came a *ski-lehrer* pulling a sledge.

'But the snow's wonderful. What rotten luck to have an accident today, and on a gentle slope like that one,' Liz exclaimed. 'Oh, I bet it's that girl.'

'What girl?' asked Patrick.

'A girl who arrived from England last night on her honeymoon. She's never ski-ed before, and when we went down earlier we saw her husband giving her a lesson just about where all that commotion is.'

'You mean he brought her up here on her first day on skis?'

'Yes. How crazy can you be? He said the nursery slopes were much too crowded and the snow up here's so perfect now. She seemed to be sliding along quite nicely.'

'How was he planning to get her to the bottom?' asked the professor. 'She couldn't have ski-ed all the way down.'

'They said they were going to climb back to the restaurant and go down in the chair,' said Francis. 'The fellow's mad, of course.'

'Some climb,' said Patrick, looking back the way they had come.

'I shouldn't care to do it,' said Liz, whose muscles always screamed after only the shortest stretch of side-stepping or herring-bone climbing.

"Well, whoever it is, there's sure to be a doctor among those people gathered round,' said Francis. 'I've seen plenty of ski-ing accidents, and each time someone you've never noticed before turns out to be a doctor.'

'Everything seems to be under control, certainly,' said Patrick. The sledge had reached the scene now, and the little crowd of people had moved back. It was possible, even through the snow that still fell lightly, to see the activity round the recumbent figure on the ground.

'Are you coming this way, Mrs. Morris?' the professor asked Liz, pointing to the start of the Red Run. His beard was covered in snowflakes, giving him a Santa Claus look.

'Good gracious, no! That would be asking for trouble,' Liz said. 'The White Run for me.'

'You could easily manage the Blue,' said Francis. 'And the Red, come to that.'

'I don't want to end up on a stretcher too,' said Liz.

'You wouldn't,' Francis told her, laughing. 'We'll do them before the holiday ends. Come on, then. Shall I go first?'

He started off, and Liz followed, wavering a bit while she felt that Patrick was watching, but soon steadying.

'A charming woman,' said the professor.

Patrick supposed that she was.

He enjoyed his own trip down the Red Run. It was quite challenging, since Max went very fast, but the snow was good and his skis bit sharply into it; areas that would have been ice traps in other conditions were not alarming. It was quiet in the woods, with just the sound of the snow hissing beneath their skis. Patrick concentrated on his movements, not wanting to fall again. They crossed the hanging bridge above the Gentiana and ski-ed on, past the hotel and into the village, until the slope ended. Then they stopped, unclipped their skis, shouldered them, and walked towards the centre of Greutz. By this time it was warmer again, and the snow was falling more heavily.

'How about a beer?' Patrick suggested. 'Let me buy you one. Where shall we go?'

They went into the Silvretta bar, and found Sue and the Dutchman seated there already, looking rather glum; Jan was drinking beer and Sue had a *gluwein* before her. Max and Patrick joined them.

'What's up, Sue? You do look miserable,' Patrick asked.

'June Foster, that English girl who arrived last night, has broken her leg,' Sue answered. She was playing with a packet of sugar, a small square of sealed paper printed with a picture of edelweiss. 'Jan and I met the blood-wagon outside the clinic.'

'So Liz was right. We met her up at Obergreutz,' said Patrick. 'We could see someone had had an accident. Liz was afraid it might be this girl.'

'Sue, you have so tender a heart,' Jan told her, patting her hand and gazing earnestly into her eyes. Patrick thought it was as well Liz was not there to witness this touching scene.

'What a misfortune,' said the professor. 'But the patient will be in good hands in the clinic. Dr. Wesser is expert with fractures.'

'I'm sure he is,' said Patrick feelingly. He must get plenty of practice.

'How did it happen, do you know?' asked the professor.

'She ran off the *piste* into the deep snow,' said Jan. 'And she was very tired, too.'

'Oh, is that what happened?' asked Sue.

'I heard the *lehrers* talking,' Jan explained. 'They were angry because she was up there, a beginner. She had got tired, of course, as one does. And I suppose no one told her to be careful to stay on the *piste*. I, alas, am always running off it and falling down, but I bounce.'

'I'd forgotten you speak German,' Sue said.

'Most Dutch people do,' said Jan. 'And English, too. Our country is so small, and our own language is so difficult, that we have to learn others.'

'And you were occupied during the war,' Patrick observed.

'That too,' Jan agreed. 'I was a child then. My friends and I put sand in the petrol tanks of German lorries.'

'Did you? Weren't you caught?'

'Luckily not. I was not so large in those days,' he said.

Sue glanced at Max, and with the bluntness that was the despair of her friends said, 'You must have had a terrible time in the war, Professor.'

'I did, Miss Carter,' Max said simply. 'My wife was Jewish, and I had many Jewish friends who disappeared. I was imprisoned for a time myself, because of this, but later I was released because my knowledge of England was useful.'

If Sue were not so pretty she would never get away with her naïvety, thought Patrick, racking his brains for a way of changing the subject before she went too far.

'You didn't want to get away after the war?' asked Jan.

'I spent two years in the United States,' Max answered. 'Then I came back. I wanted to repair some of the damage. One has great influence when one comes in contact with the young, as I have done all this time. The future belongs to the young now.'

Max's young wife and baby daughter had been killed in Ravensbruck, Patrick knew. He had never really got over this tragedy, any more than a man who lost his sight got over that, though he might accept it.

'Max and I thoroughly enjoyed ourselves last night, Sue,' Patrick said firmly. 'Didn't we, Max?'

'Indeed it was a great pleasure,' agreed the professor. 'You were all so hospitable. I wonder if you would give me the pleasure of returning your kindness by coming to my chalet this evening? You, Miss Carter, and Mynheer van Hutter, and Mrs. Morris, and all your charming friends whom I met last night.'

'What, all of us?' Sue asked.

'Yes, indeed. Mr. and Mrs. Whittaker, is that correct? And the German lady; and Mr. Irwin, the actor. And the young lady in the green mantle too, if she would care to come. Your courier. Patrick and I met her in the hall.'

'It's very kind of you,' said Sue. 'I'm sure we'd all love to come. May I accept and bring as many people as are free?'

'Do so, please. And the unfortunate husband of the invalid, too, if he would like to join us,' said the professor.

'I expect he'll be with June at the clinic. But I'll pass on your invitation, with pleasure,' Sue said. How nice. A little jaunt to bridge the gap between tea and dinner. 'Here comes Roy Foster now,' she added, gazing past Patrick to the door. 'And my goodness, look who's with him! Some people don't waste any time.'

Patrick glanced at the two newcomers. He had not met Roy, who at first cursory inspection looked rather ordinary, like plenty of other young men: slightly shaggy about the head, a bit too heavy for his age, and physically robust. But there was no doubt about the identity of his companion. There could not be two red heads like that in Greutz today; it was Fiona.

## II

Liz was in a bad temper by the evening, when it was time to go to Professor Klocker's. She spent half an hour in the hotel lounge after lunch, with a book. In their corner the usual bridge four of the Whittakers, Sam Irwin and Frau Hiller had settled for the afternoon; her eyes were drawn to them as if by a magnet, and she wondered about Francis. She still did not know what work he did. Was he enjoying himself now, intent on the cards, or was this the price exacted for the morning's freedom? Having failed with her own marriage, she was morbidly fascinated by the management of other people's, and his conversation had made her still more curious. After a while she could bear it no longer, so she went upstairs and lay on her bed, reading. Sue was out, swimming with Jan at the Grand Hotel.

Liz grew drowsy over her book; it was snug in the warm room, with the snow coming down hard outside, and soon she could not keep her eyes open. She slept for over an hour, and woke feeling heavy in the head and thoroughly depressed. The return of Sue in giggly high spirits did not improve Liz's humour.

The village looked ghostly as they walked through it to the professor's chalet. The snow still fell, soft and silent; it was warmer again and through the huge white flakes lights shone out from windows on their way. At the sides of the road the great banks of snow left by the ploughs towered above their heads. Near the church, Liz and Sue caught up the Whittakers and Frau Hiller, who was out of breath with the climb, panting and laughing. She said something in German as they all met.

'Frau Hiller says playing bridge is no proper training for mountain-climbing,' Francis translated. He answered her in English, telling her that she would soon be fit when the rink was cleared and she could spend all day curling, as she had intended when she came to Greutz. He took the German woman's arm, and they fell back a little behind the other three, walking more slowly up the incline.

Professor Klocker greeted them, dressed in a green velvet smoking jacket and a maroon cravat. He looked very distinguished, Liz thought, and said so to Patrick.

'He is very distinguished,' Patrick replied. 'He lectures all over the world. But his subject is English, just think of that. He talks about great English dramatists, doesn't that stir your national pride?'

'You forget that I have a degree in English,' Liz answered haughtily. 'You don't have to sell our literature to me.'

Sam Irwin and Jan had already arrived. The Dutchman greeted Sue with controlled rapture; though they had parted only a short time before, after their swim, they still seemed to have plenty to discuss and drifted together into a corner of the room. Sam had been talking to Patrick when the others arrived, and they now resumed their interrupted conversation.

'I shall come and see you,' Patrick said. 'I'll bring Liz, if she's good. You're another upholder of our heritage.'

'Where will you take me?' Liz asked suspiciously. 'What's this all about?'

'Nothing's fixed for certain yet. It may never happen,' Sam said, deprecatingly. 'The whole thing could fall through.'

'Nonsense,' said Patrick roundly. 'This is the start of better things. He's playing Sir Andrew in a new *Twelfth Night*,' he added to Liz.

'It's only a provincial tour with a repertory company,' Sam said. 'It won't amount to much.'

'It may lead to a very great deal,' said Patrick. 'What a pity you didn't get Malvolio, though.'

'Oh well. One can't have everything,' Sam said. 'This will be quite a challenge.' He set his jaw, and Liz noticed how his face, which she had hitherto considered had an unformed look, strengthened. 'I don't know what line the direction's going to take, but one can do quite a lot with poor Sir Andrew.'

'Patrick told me how much he admired your work,' Liz said.

Sam looked pleased.

'I'm surprised anyone remembers it,' he said. 'It's a long time since I did anything worthwhile.'

'Do you enjoy modern drama?' asked Liz. 'What about all this stripping? It must be so draughty.'

Sam gave a wry smile. He never seemed to laugh.

'I once played Ariel, rather bare except for a lot of green paint,' he said. 'Otherwise I've managed to keep covered. Unfortunately one can't be choosy nowadays, but if I had the option I'd always pick a period piece rather than anything contemporary.'

'Why? Can't you identify with the present age, or do you just like dressing up?' Liz asked, and was surprised when he looked discomfited. But he answered calmly.

'A bit of both, I think. Clothes help one to asume the character.'

'Who is to be Malvolio?' Patrick asked.

Sam did not know.

They talked about the play a little longer and then, with a mumbled excuse, Sam drifted away to join the Whittakers.

'What an odd creature he is,' said Liz. 'That's the longest conversation I've ever had with him. Did you see how embarrassed he looked when I said in the nicest way he might be square?'

'I didn't think that was what had touched him,' Patrick answered. 'You also suggested that he might enjoy dressing up.'

Liz stared.

'Well, he does, of course. All men do. Look at you, dons love wearing their robes. And judges too, and field-marshals and so on. What's sinister in that? It's merely childish.'

'I love you, Liz. You're still so innocent,' said Patrick gently.

'And you are vile,' Liz told him crossly. 'How can you know about Sam? You've scarcely met him.'

'I don't, I'm only needling you,' said Patrick.

But Liz was looking at Sam across the room.

'You could be right, at that,' she said slowly. 'He likes Barbara, but he avoids Sue and me like the plague. I thought it was just normal male conceit, imagining we'd waste our time on him.'

'You're quite a fetching pair of birds, you know,' Patrick remarked. 'You'd come quite easily between most men and their sleep. A menace to the vulnerable.'

Which he most certainly was not. The trouble about Patrick's theories was that even if he uttered them merely to provoke, they were based on possibility and lingered in the mind. Liz gazed at Sam.

'Poor fellow,' said Patrick. 'Don't keep looking at him. He'll really think he's made his mark, one way or another.'

'I don't think he's anything in particular,' Liz declared. 'He's just a flabby "don't-know", who needs someone to write a part for him.'

'You may be right,' said Patrick. 'How's Sue getting on over there? She seems a bit smitten with that Dutchman.'

'I'm afraid she is. She can never resist an opportunity,' Liz sighed. 'It always ends in tears.'

'She mends quite quickly, doesn't she?' said Patrick, sadly lacking in sympathy.

'She needs a lot of glueing up each time,' Liz said.

'And what about you, old dear?'

Liz had been looking at Francis while they talked. She turned away hastily. Patrick saw too much.

'I'm giving up men,' she said lightly. 'I'm such a rotten picker.'

'Don't do that, Liz,' said Patrick. 'That's the coward's way.'

'Much you know about it.'

'I know more than you think,' said Patrick, watching her.

'Oh Patrick, if the weather doesn't get better soon we'll all explode,' Liz burst out suddenly. For there was another week ahead. 'I love a ski-ing holiday, because there's plenty to do and it's nice to be out of England during February. But to be cooped up in this tiny place with these dreadful weather conditions and all these ferments – God!'

'What ferments, love?' Patrick asked her. 'I see only minor ones around us – Sue smirking at her Dutchman, and Irwin, whatever his phobia may be, just anxious about his sword-play with Sebastian in Illyria, and Max bothered about the last chapter of his book. The Whittakers are busy being kind to a German lady to show there's no ill-will, and she's intent on letting them be kind for the same reason. Everyone's calm. Aren't you?'

'No, I'm not, and you know it,' Liz said. 'Get me some more of this drink, Patrick, it seems very powerful and I need it. This holiday's turning me into a toper.'

As Patrick obeyed her, Penny arrived; she had been visiting June at the clinic, and disclosed that she had found the wounded one in tears because Roy had not been near her since the accident.

'It's bad, isn't it?' Penny said. 'I'm not surprised she's miserable.' She accepted a drink, and looked round the room. 'Where's Bernard? Isn't he coming?' she asked.

No one knew. A note had been left for him at the hotel, passing on the professor's invitation since it included the whole British contingent in the Gentiana. The Derringtons had an engagement with friends at the Silvretta and had not come.

'Who is Bernard?' Patrick wanted to know.

'An insignificant fellow who scuttles about like the White Rabbit hurrying to keep mysterious appointments,' Liz said.

'Would that be the chap in galoshes who came into the hotel just as Max and I were leaving last night?'

'Galoshes? Was he wearing galoshes?' Liz said. 'It sounds like him.'

'He's a solicitor, isn't he?' Sue asked.

'He's clerk to the Wapshot town council,' said Sam.

'He skis in all weathers, he's my keenest client,' Penny said. 'But the Derringtons will challenge him. They've spent the whole afternoon going up and down the Blue Run. The Red's closed now.'

'The Derringtons run a mink farm near Maidstone,' Liz told Patrick, to show she kept up with the news.

'I'm so sorry that not all your group is here,' the professor said.

'You've got quite enough of us as it is,' said Sue, 'and if this weather goes on you'll meet us all far too many times.'

'It cannot be too often for me, Miss Carter,' the professor replied gallantly. 'Just as long as I finish my book on time.'

'Max is writing a book about Marlowe, and it's totally new, not one he's already written six times before under different titles, like so many scholars,' said Patrick, grinning.

'Did he and was he,' said Sam to himself.

'Did he and was he what?' asked Sue.

'Was he Shakespeare, I suppose is what Sam meant,' said Liz. 'But of course he wasn't, otherwise what was Shakespeare doing all that time?'

'I thought Marlowe died young,' remarked Francis.

'He did.'

'People think perhaps he didn't, and was scribbling away busily instead,' Liz enlarged. 'While Shakespeare merely acted.'

Someone mentioned Bacon, and Patrick told Liz under cover

of the talk that he was pleased to see her spirits were returning. She glowered at him.

'You're the most appalling intellectual snob,' she said. 'At least he's heard of Marlowe. There are heaps of quite nice chaps who haven't.'

'I don't believe you,' Patrick said. He was laughing at her. She felt like hitting him with any handy weapon.

'Let's find out the answer to our bet,' Patrick now said. 'I suppose you didn't discover it this morning when you were skylarking on the mountain?'

'No, I did not,' Liz snapped. 'We had other things to think about, and after that girl broke her leg we followed her down and took her skis back to the hotel and fetched her nightdress and so on.'

'What was her husband doing?'

'He vanished. It's a good thing he didn't show up here this evening, I'd have given him a piece of my mind.'

'Perhaps he can't stand the sight of blood.'

'There wasn't any. Just a groan or two. They gave her some dope before they brought her down. Poor silly girl.'

'Why do you call her silly?'

'Because she's made such a ghastly marriage.'

'Perhaps they deserve each other. People sometimes do.'

'No one her age can merit such callous treatment,' said Liz, setting her mouth in a stubborn line.

This was dangerous ground, and Patrick sheered away.

'Come on. Let's tackle Whittaker,' he said. 'We'll try a diversion.'

Max was still talking about Marlowe to an audience of the Whittakers, Frau Hiller and Sam Irwin. Like anyone well launched into their own subject, he was happy; Sam prompted him now and then with apt queries, and Frau Hiller, concentrating hard, seemed interested, but Barbara's face wore a glazed look. She and Francis seized on the appearance of Patrick and Liz to break away, and Barbara moved off to talk to Penny.

Patrick used the old gambit of asking Francis where he lived.

'In Dorset, not far from Charmouth,' Francis answered.

'A beautiful part of the world, and with most romantic associations,' Patrick said.

He was getting pompous, and much too donnish, Liz thought.

'You mean because of Charles II?' she said.

'Who else?' said Patrick loftily. 'Alas, poor Limbry. What a tale of might-have-been.'

Liz had been thinking of Hardy, but on reflection wondered if his country was not further east than Charmouth. She would not hazard the topic in front of Patrick, who would crow if he caught her out. But she did not know who Limbry was, and felt obliged to ask.

Francis supplied the answer, and great was her delight at having the wind thus taken out of Patrick's sails, for she knew he was surprised that Francis could do it.

'He was the master of the ship that was supposed to take Charles to France, but never turned up. He told his wife he was going to carry a dangerous cargo, and she locked him up until he promised not to go,' he told her.

"That district's over-run by tourists in the summer, isn't it?' Patrick said. 'It must be irritating if you live there. All those caravans in colonies.'

'I'm afraid I run one of those colonies,' Francis disclosed, with a rueful smile.

'Do you?' Liz was astounded. In a hundred years, as she told Patrick later, she would never have guessed that this was his job.

'Mine isn't one of those cliff-top fields with rank upon rank of vans in rows like a housing estate,' Francis said. 'We have twelve acres with woodlands and a small lake, and the vans are sited among the trees. We've only got thirty, and some cottages and flats too, which we let.'

'Rather exclusive then?' said Patrick.

'I hope so,' Francis agreed. 'My wife's parents had this lovely old house, which we didn't want to sell after they died. Unfortunately they didn't leave enough money to run it, so we had to make it work for us. We decided that this was a safer way than market gardening, or turning it into a hotel.'

'You've no catering problems, anyway,' said Patrick.

'Exactly. The main work is maintenance. I spend the winter doing the repairs and so on that are necessary before the season starts.'

That explained the calloused hands.

'It keeps me tied there in the summer, but it's so pleasant that I never want to leave then,' he went on. 'Barbara usually goes away for a while; she does get bothered by the visitors. After all, it was her home.'

'How long have you been doing this?' asked Liz.

'Five years, since I left the army. This will be the sixth summer.'

'Have you any family?' Patrick inquired.

'A daughter. She's still at school.'

Once again Liz had a surprise. Barbara did not fit her picture of a maternal woman and she had made up her mind that they had no children. But Francis was continuing. 'My first wife died when Jill was two,' he said. Worse and worse : seeking only a little information, she now had far too much for her volatile imagination to digest.

But Patrick was bringing them back to mundane matters.

'That coast is very stony. Isn't Charmouth the only sandy beach for miles?'

'You're quite right,' Francis confirmed. 'It's an area that gets a lot of sea mists, too, unfortunately.'

'And smugglers,' Liz said, wildly. 'I mean, there must have been.'

'I shouldn't be surprised if there aren't a few still,' said Francis, with a smile. 'Perhaps further west, where there are wide river mouths.'

He was not laughing at her, Liz knew, but she was less sure of his attitude to Patrick; there was an ambivalence about his answers to Patrick's probing that made her wonder. Her loyalties swung back and forth : she could laugh at Patrick herself, and scold him, too; but she grew angry at the idea that others might react to him the same way. He was wise and astute; she trusted him, and would permit no one but herself to mock him.

He seemed, however, to have noticed nothing amiss; in a most amicable manner he and Francis were discussing sailing, and the tides around Lyme Bay. Liz decided that the weather was having a very peculiar effect on her.

Eventually it was time to return to the Gentiana. When they left the chalet, in a cheerful group, it was snowing as hard as ever, and the path so lately cut to the professor's door had vanished under a thick layer of new snow. The village, as they walked through it, was deserted; everyone else was at dinner.

In the Gentiana restaurant the Derringtons had reached the dessert; Roy Foster had finished his meal and gone, to visit June it was to be hoped; but Bernard's place was still laid.

'Where can he be?' wondered Penny. 'He's usually so punctual.' She asked the Derringtons if they had seen him.

'Who? B. Walker, you mean?' asked Hilda, holding up his napkin in its hessian folder and reading the name that was printed on its label. 'Have we met him?'

'You must have done. He's here at meals,' said Penny.

'Well, he wasn't at breakfast,' Hilda said. 'Oh, do you mean the middle-aged schoolboy with glasses and curls who was making a pass at Fiona last night?'

'Er – yes. Except that she was making the pass, not him,' said Penny.

'Haven't seen him since,' said Freddie, spooning up peach melba. 'Have you, Hilda?'

'Not a sign.'

'Maybe he's still on the job,' sniggered Freddie.

'Fiona – ' Sue paused. She had been going to say that Fiona certainly was not.

'Fiona's had dinner,' Penny pointed out. 'Her place has been cleared.'

She could have eaten with Roy, Sue thought. And they could be together now; there was no sound of music echoing up from the cellar yet.

'Are you dancing tonight?' asked Freddie. He addressed Sue, across the table.

'Yes.' Jan was coming over after his meal at the Silvretta. Sue forgot Bernard; it was so nice to have something pleasant to anticipate.

'Good. We're going down too,' Freddie said. He winked at Sue. 'We'll show 'em, eh, Sue?'

'What? Oh, will we?' Sue was taken aback.

'I'm not dancing. I'm going to wash my hair,' said Penny, as the Derringtons left. 'It's odd about Bernard. I suppose he'll turn up. There's a tummy bug about, perhaps he's got that.'

'Maybe he has,' said Sue, watching Freddie depart. How gratifying not to need him to dance with tonight. She ate on, with appetite.

Liz, sourly cutting up her pork, thought she would spend the evening discussing Wagner or some other equally erudite topic with Frau Hiller, in splendid feminine isolation.

## PART FOUR

# Monday

## I

In the end Liz went to the discotheque with the others, but she stayed only a short time. It was stuffy in the smoky atmosphere, and she had not enjoyed the spectacle of Roy Foster and Fiona glued together throughout the evening, except when she prised herself away from him for just long enough to change the records.

Sue came up very late; as she undressed, trying to move quietly, she kept giggling to herself. Liz, feigning sleep, hid her face in the thick *duvet* and sighed inwardly. Jan and Sue must have managed to find some cosy private corner; the ski-room, perhaps. If only Sue could meet someone who would marry her, how much better it would be, but she never seemed to click with bachelors. As for herself, she was content, she told herself firmly. She had a worthwhile job through which she met many interesting people on an unemotional level, and that satisfied her. Yet here she was, regretting that she had not stayed in the nightclub long enough that evening to have another chance of dancing with Francis. It must be the altitude.

Just as Sue got into bed, Liz spoke.

'Did Bernard turn up?'

'Why didn't you say you were awake?' demanded Sue, who had stubbed her toe on the bedstead. 'I've been creeping about trying not to disturb you, and now I've hurt myself.'

'Did he?' Liz persisted.

'I didn't see him,' said Sue crossly. 'Anyway, who cares?'

At breakfast, Bernard's place was still empty.

'He always used to be first down,' said Sam. 'I expect the weather's got into him. Frau Scholler was saying that over fifty centimetres of snow fell in the night.'

The weather that was making most people feel edgy seemed to be mellowing Sam. He looked relaxed and happy this morning, spreading the pale unsalted butter thickly on his dreary bread.

Penny was over at the Whittakers' table talking to them earnestly. She came back to her own place and poursed herself out some more coffee.

'Now who haven't I seen?' she said, looking round at her assembled clients. 'Sue and Liz – you weren't down when I told the others. No one may go further than the end of the village, and you mustn't go along the Kramms road at all. Is that quite clear? We're all right here, in the Gentiana, and the village is safe, but there's a danger spot on the Kramms road, in the gulley where the little fall was on Saturday night. It's just a safety precaution, the burgomeister's orders. There hasn't been an avalanche in Greutz for years and years.'

'No ski-ing,' Freddie said glumly.

'I'm meeting the other couriers later. We'll lay on a snowball fight, Hickson's versus Snopranx,' Penny said. 'And perhaps we could fix a ping-pong tournament this afternoon.'

Sam shuddered.

'Not for me, Penny,' he said. 'Maybe Bernard will volunteer for your team. Where can he have got to?'

'Has no one really seen him?' Penny asked. 'He must be just having a lie-in.'

'I didn't see him at all yesterday. Did he have any of his meals?' said Sue.

'Did anyone see him?'

No one had.

'He's probably not well, or sulking,' Penny said. 'The weather's getting tons of people down. Several marriages are tottering at the Silvretta. Thank goodness they're Snopranx people, not my lot. Still, I'll ask Else if she's seen him.'

She called the waitress over and spoke to her in German. The girl shook her head, and answered briefly.

'Else says he didn't come for any of his meals yesterday,' said Penny.

'That doesn't mean a thing. He's probably got tired of the food here and is eating out,' said Hilda.

'Not Bernard. Not when he's already paid for his meals here,' said Sue. 'He counts up every *schilling*.'

'He must be ill,' said Liz. 'We'd better go and see.'

'I'll go,' Sam offered. 'His room's near mine. He'll curse me, no doubt, but we'd better sort this out, if you're all going to worry.'

'He may have a girl up there,' said Freddie.

'Very funny,' said Sue. 'You obviously don't know our Bernard.'

Sam went off. He returned quite quickly, and now he did look concerned.

'He isn't in his room, and his bed hasn't been slept in,' he said.

'He's probably with a bird in another hotel,' said Roy Foster, who had so far made no contribution to the conversation. He looked pale, and had drunk three cups of strong coffee without eating anything, clearly suffering from a monumental hang-over.

'Still waters run deep, we know, but not as deep as that,' said Sue cryptically. 'Where on earth can he be?'

By this time the Whittakers had finished their breakfast. As on the previous day, Barbara left the dining-room, but Francis came to join the others. He pulled up a chair and sat beside Liz.

'What's up? You all look very worried,' he said. 'We're safe enough here from avalanches.'

'It isn't that. Bernard Walker seems to have vanished,' said Penny.

'He can't have. What makes you think so?'

'No one seems to have seen him since – when? Did you see him on the Schneiderhorn yesterday? He never misses a day's ski-ing.'

'I didn't see him yesterday, but that doesn't signify,' said Francis. 'I wouldn't be looking out for him.'

'He ski-ed alone a lot. He used to go up when the class had

finished and do an extra run. If he did that yesterday, just before the lifts stopped, and fell – ' Sam did not finish.

'But the *lehrers* go down all the runs after the last person,' said Freddie. 'At least, they do everywhere else. They must do it here too.'

'Oh yes, they do,' said Penny. 'But suppose he'd run off the *piste*?'

'Someone would have seen him. Or heard him, he'd have yelled,' said Roy.

'He might have knocked himself out. Or got buried in a drift,' said Penny.

'Well, cheer up. We're not certain he's missing yet,' said Freddie. 'Mark my words, in spite of what you say, he'll have spent the night with a girl somewhere, and he won't be too pleased if there's a hue and cry. After all, what else is left but sex in this sort of weather?'

'There's always bridge,' said Liz tartly.

'Well, if you're going to send out a search-party, let us know, and we'll join in,' said Hilda, getting up. 'Meanwhile, I am going to have my hair done.'

'I'm off too,' said Roy, rising.

'Have you heard how June is this morning?' Sue asked him.

'Not yet.'

'Well, give her our love.'

'I'll do that.'

He and the Derringtons left, and Penny turned worriedly to the others.

'Now what should I do about Bernard?' she asked their advice. 'I'd better consult Frau Scholler. We don't want to start a panic. Freddie may be quite right. He was always rushing off to keep appointments, but he never said who with. Even if he isn't with a girl he may be with some crony we don't know about, and stayed the night rather than walk back here with it snowing so hard.'

'Would you like some support, Penny? I'll come with you if you like,' Francis offered.

Penny looked grateful.

'Yes, please,' she said. She and Francis went off and the others continued silently with breakfast. It seemed a wild idea that anything should have happened to Bernard but Penny's suggestion made good sense; everyone had heard Bernard's remarks about having to meet people.

Francis came back and told them that the Schollers were organising a discreet inquiry round the hotels.

'Penny's going to talk to the other couriers. Someone's sure to have seen him,' he continued. 'I'm going to find the people in his ski-class to see where he went yesterday, or if they know who his friends are. It's probably all a storm in a tea-cup and he'll walk in for lunch as right as rain.'

His words made sense, but there was still a feeling of uneasiness among the others after he had gone. They drifted out into the hall where they stood about looking through the swing doors at the yellow-tinged world outside where the snow still fell gently. Sam went over to the annexe where he found the maid who cleaned his room and Bernard's. She told him in her halting English that though Bernard's bed had been rumpled the day before, as if someone had lain on it, his pyjamas had been left still as she had laid them out for him the evening before, a task she carried out while the guests were dining.

'Of course it doesn't prove anything,' Sam added, after he had related this to the others.

'It could mean he was missing all day yesterday,' Liz said sharply.

'We're already afraid of that, aren't we?' Sam answered her.

'We should have noticed,' Liz insisted.

'We're not his keepers, have some sense,' said Sue. 'Well, we can't spend the morning standing here. I shall take a tip from Hilda and have my hair done. What about you, Liz?'

'I couldn't sit still,' Liz replied. 'You go. I'll have a walk, at least as far as one's allowed.' The permitted area must surely extend to the professor's chalet. A dose of Patrick might get things in proportion.

It was still very muggy out of doors, and everything was hushed. People were walking carefully, as if they feared incautious treading might set off enough vibrations to dislodge the menacing snow piled on the mountain tops. Liz had loved the mountains since her first sight of Mont Blanc, pink-tipped at dawn, when she was a schoolgirl, but today she hated them. Climatic conditions did profound things to people's temperaments, and here was nature manifestly still untamed. She longed suddenly for the neat fields of England and her own civilised flat in Bolton Gardens.

At the end of the Gentiana lane, instead of going towards the village she turned to the right along the Kramms road, and walked on until, quite quickly, she came to a barricade made of barbed wire with a mandatory notice attached, printed in red in several languages, forbidding further progress. Having inspected that, she turned back and walked into the village. Near the bridge she stood by the river's edge, looking at the water. It was sluggish, black, mysterious. Across on the far bank was the clinic, an austere, concrete-faced building with balconies to many of the windows. In there poor June must be lying with her Potts fracture now pinned and in plaster. It depressed Liz still more to contemplate her plight. She ought to visit her; Sue already had, the afternoon before.

She walked on up the road, to the Grand Hotel, and beyond it until she met another barrier like the one below; then she retraced her steps and set off up the slope past the church to Professor Klocker's chalet.

Patrick opened the door to her.

'A woman! Just what we need!' he cried. 'Come in, Liz, and welcome. Helga's marooned in Kramms, where she went last night to visit her daughter, and Max and I are left fending for ourselves. Rescue us, I implore you.'

'Do you mean to say your brilliant brains can't direct themselves to a little domesticity?' asked Liz caustically.

'You forget how cossetted we both are. I never do more than make tea or Nescafé at Mark's, and Max has a replica of Helga in Innsbruck, anticipating his every need.'

'Idiot. I'm perfectly aware that you can cook sausages,' said Liz, thinking back to a May morning a long time ago.

'There are no humble bangers in Greutz,' Patrick told her. 'The local kind are much more sophisticated. But all this merry banter is merely a ruse to prevent me from bursting with delight because you're obviously unable to keep away from me.' He took her anorak from her, shook it in a housewifely fashion outside the front door, pointed at her snowy boots, and before she could take them off held her by either arm and kissed her. She suddenly clung to him. He was familiar : tiresome, indeed exasperating; but safe.

'Liz dear!' he exclaimed, hugging her with warmth but detaching her slightly so that he could inspect her face. She was almost in tears. 'Whatever's wrong? Shall I run the fellow through for you?'

Liz made an effort to regain control and laughed shakily.

'It hasn't come to that,' she said. 'I'm a fool and a clot, but I don't seem to be quite myself, what with one thing and another. Patrick, one of the guests at the Gentiana has disappeared.'

'Not the one you've a yen for? Not Whittaker?'

So Patrick had noticed. He knew her much too well. She simply shook her head.

'Well, that's something anyway. Come and tell me all about it,' he said.

'Let me take my boots off first,' said Liz. She sniffed, and like a child rubbed her face on the sleeve of her thick sweater.

'You are in a way, aren't you? Never mind the boots, I was only fooling.'

'I know, but there's no point in making pools of water everywhere,' she said. 'Where's the professor? Cooking lunch?'

'No. He's working on his book, he's miles away with Marlowe,' said Patrick. 'He won't have heard us. Come into the kitchen and talk to me there.'

Liz was not so far gone in woe that she failed to be amused by Patrick's arrangements. Neatly aligned on a board by the stove were two flattened slices of veal fillet, some chopped mushrooms in a heap, chopped onions, and a packet of frozen peas. The table was spread with a red and white checked cloth; bread, cheese and butter were laid ready, and a bottle of wine stood open on the draining board.

'You'd make a dear little wife,' she said.

'That's better. There's hope if you can still smile,' said Patrick.

He opened a cupboard and took out a bottle of rum, and poured her out a tot. 'Max has got the rest of the drink in his study, we won't disturb him while he's working, he's got some deadline with his publisher for this book. Rum's a pretty good restorative. Swallow it down and tell me all,' he commanded.

They sat on either side of the table and Liz related what was known about Bernard thus far.

'But, my love, you're jumping to conclusions. He's probably bedded down with some curvy female for the duration of the snow-in,' said Patrick when she had finished.

'You haven't met him, at least not to talk to. He isn't like that. Anyone else, maybe; even you, though I sometimes wonder. But not Bernard.'

'I'll ignore the implied insult,' Patrick said with dignity. 'Let's stick to the matter in hand. Do you mean that he's queer? Maybe he's with a fellow, then.'

'No, I don't think he is queer. I don't even think he's one of those neuter types who's neither one thing or the other – which incidentally I think describes Sam, not what you implied, if I understood you. I think Bernard's someone who'd like to, but doesn't dare. Hilda Derrington described him as a middle-aged schoolboy, which was rather shrewd of her, especially as she'd only met him once. He's never in one place for long, always darting off to keep some undisclosed date, but I've never seen him dancing, or even talking to a girl, except when he literally can't help it. He was entwined with Fiona in the nightclub on Saturday, after you left, but she was making the running. She was completely plastered, I don't supose she knew whose neck she was draped around. Bernard looked most uncomfortable.' Liz described the scene. 'I think all the running about he does is an act – to seem busy.'

'Did they leave together? Fiona and Bernard?'

'I don't know. I didn't stay to see. Sue was loitering about with her Dutchman and I left first.'

'Ahead of the others? The Whittakers and Irwin?'

'Yes, but I don't think they were far behind me. What does it matter?'

'It doesn't yet. I don't suppose Fiona has vanished too?'

'No, she hasn't. She's done a transference to Roy Foster, the one whose wife has broken her leg.'

'Hm.' Patrick poured her out some more rum. 'Let me know if he's still missing after lunch and I'll come over.'

'But what can you do? If he's lost on the mountain there isn't a hope for him. No one could even begin to look for him in these conditions. If he had a fall, he'd be buried – you know what it's like if you come off a drag or something into the deep snow, it's almost impossible to get out. If he was up on the mountain all night – well.'

'He's probably safe and warm in some snug hut,' said Patrick. 'The altitude or the weather, or both, are playing tricks with your mind, my love.' He spoke gently, and held her hand across the table.

'Oh Patrick, why on earth can't I be in love with you? At least then I'd know where I was!' she cried despairingly.

'Darling Liz, you know I'm devoted to you, so please feel free to use me as a prophylactic, which I think is what you need,' he told her gravely. 'Fall for me, by all means, while the dangerous infection is abroad, just for a week or two.'

She looked down at their joined hands. Then she freed her own.

'One day you'll fall yourself,' she said. 'And for someone who won't give two hoots for you.'

'Maybe I shall. And you will comfort me,' said Patrick.

## II

Bernard was not back by lunch-time, nor was there any news of him from the village. It was now officially conceded that there was cause for concern. In spite of the weather, the *ski-lehrers* were going up the mountain to search for him.

The Gentiana group watched the men start up on the chair-lift; they went at great risk to themselves on the loosely packed, soft snow.

'Wouldn't you know Bernard would be the one to cause trouble?' Sue said.

'I think it's so dreadful that we didn't miss him sooner,' Penny answered. 'I should have noticed yesterday.'

'Surely counting heads isn't among your duties?' Liz remarked. 'It's a reflection on him that we didn't realise earlier; he's so insignificant.'

'There's always someone like him on a tour,' Penny said. 'A bachelor, not young any more, who won't join in anything. One wonders why they come.'

'To be able to talk about it afterwards,' said Liz. 'Boasting at the office. He probably makes out that he's a hell of a chap away from home.'

'Do you think that's it?' said Penny. 'How peculiar. It can't be much fun.'

'Some people don't know how to be happy,' Francis said.

'Or how to recognise it if they are,' amplified Liz.

'Or haven't learned to equate absence of misery with contentment,' Sam contributed, hunching his lean shoulders and staring out of the huge lounge window where they were all gathered having coffee.

'That's rather a negative view, isn't it?' said Francis.

'Most of us have to settle for it, don't we?' Sam replied. 'It's the only way to live.'

'It sounds a rather dismal recipe to me, if you want my opinion,' Sue declared.

'I agree with Sam,' said Liz. 'Most of us start out with impossible expectations.'

'It's horrible to think Bernard may be somewhere up there on the mountain,' Penny said, more concerned with the immediate problem. 'Even if he was a bit of a drip, it's still awful.'

'Yes, it is,' agreed Barbara. Even she, who had so far seemed unaffected by the weather, now looked pale and drawn.

'Let's go down to the village. At least we'll be on the spot there if there's any news,' said Sue. 'We can't stay here brooding and philosophising till it's time for tea.'

All agreed that this was a good idea, and went away to fetch coats and boots. Frau Hiller, who had been listening to their conversation without joining in, said she would stay behind; the others all set off in a group.

The sight of the chair-lift working had filled some other visitors with hope that ski-ing was to be allowed after all, and they had gone hopefully to the terminus, only to be turned back. Apart from them, few people were about.

'We shouldn't be being so discreet,' Liz said suddenly. 'We ought to ask every single person we meet if they've seen him. I know all the hotels have been questioned, but there are lots of chalets and things. Someone may have noticed him.'

'An Englishman, not very young, yet not old, about five foot ten, with glasses, in a dark anorak and ski-pants. There are fifty of them here,' said Sam. 'I'm one – you're another,' he added to Francis. 'You're taller,' he said to Freddie Derrington, who was with them. 'But it comes to much the same thing. With hats on, we all look alike, and everyone must have been wearing goggles yesterday.'

It was true.

They reached the bridge and stood beside it, staring up at the mountain. It was impossible to make out through the murk the figures of the men searching up there. They had taken long slender poles to prod into the deep snow at the side of the *piste*, such as were used after an avalanche to find the buried victims.

Penny went off to the burgomeister's house. Liz, looking across at the row of chalets above the church, saw a solitary figure on the professor's balcony. She had telephoned Patrick before leaving the Gentiana to tell him that Bernard had not been found.

Penny came back and told them that if it were not for the avalanche risk the burgomeister would have asked for a helicopter to help in the search, but the vibration might be all that was needed to start a fall. In any case the weather was too bad and the visibility too poor for a helicopter to fly in the mountains.

Sue and Barbara decided, since they were so near, to visit June in the clinic. The Derringtons, who clearly hated to be idle, said they would walk up to the Grand for a swim. Liz, left with Francis, Sam and Penny, turned abruptly from them, saying she was going back to the hotel. She walked rapidly away before any of them could offer to go with her, head down, and gloved hands thrust into her pockets. She stared at the grimy snow forming the surface of the road as she went, and would have walked straight past Patrick if he had not hailed her.

'Why isn't your anorak red?' she demanded without preamble, for he too fitted the description of Bernard, although he was a much bigger man, in fact.

'I don't want to be mistaken for a ski-instructor, and I like to be garbed as the Dark Blue that I am,' he replied at once. 'But why do you ask?'

She told him.

'How shrewd of Irwin,' Patrick observed. 'What else is known about friend Bernard?'

'Not much. He's older than I thought at first. I put him down at about thirty-five, but he once said something about being nearly twice as old as Penny, which makes him over forty. He doesn't look it – a few frown lines on the brow, but no others much.'

'Life hasn't etched its careworn furrows yet, you imply?'

'More or less. He scuttled about so, maybe he never stopped long enough in one place for them to form.'

'Where's his room? Near yours?'

'No. It's in the annexe beyond the hotel.'

Patrick walked silently past the main building of the Gentiana, brushed his snowy boots on the annexe doorstep with the stiff broom provided, and went inside.

'Where are you going?' Liz demanded, following.

'Which is his room. Do you know?'

'You can't go into it.'

'Why not?'

'Someone may see you. And you've got no right.'

'Everyone's out, or asleep. And I'm going to look for him. He may have come back,' said Patrick. 'Which is it? Or must I try each one?'

He was perfectly capable of doing just that, and of getting away with it too.

'I think it's number three, on the first floor,' Liz said. 'I know

Sam's is four, and they're next to each other. But I wish you wouldn't, Patrick.'

He ignored her protests, merely walking firmly up the steep stairs which were covered with coconut matting. Liz followed, muttering under her breath. The key of Bernard's room hung, as in so many mountain hotels, on a hook over the door. Patrick took it down and let himself into the room; Liz went in too, and he closed the door behind them.

It was the usual small slit of a room, perfectly adequate but not luxurious. There was a washbasin, a varnished pine wardrobe, a bedside cabinet, a table covered with a white cloth, and an upright chair. There were big double windows, but no balcony.

'They never give you a dressing-table, do they? Must be tough on you girls with all your pots and jars,' said Patrick. On Bernard's table was a pair of brushes with yellowed ivory backs and dingy bristles. They bore a monogram : DBW.

'His Dad's, at a guess,' said Patrick.

There were a book of crossword puzzles, two picture postcards addressed and stamped but with the correspondence side still blank, and a week-old copy of the *Sunday Telegraph* also on the table. On the shelf over the basin there were a bottle of Steradent, a toothbrush, a tube of toothpaste and some shaving cream, a piece of old soap, a worn shaving-brush and a safety razor. Patrick opened the wardrobe. One side of it was fitted with shelves, and here, tidily arranged, was a rather grubby pale blue polo-necked cotton shirt, a Norwegian-knit sweater in grey and white, a woollen vest and a pair of pants, two pairs of socks and some white cotton handkerchiefs. A pair of grey flannels hung on a hanger.

'He wasn't wearing this sweater on Saturday evening?' Patrick asked.

'No. He's got another, black and white, it looks new. This is his day-time one.'

'Shoes,' said Patrick, looking down. On the floor of the cupboard stood Bernard's ski-boots. There were no other shoes, not even a pair of bedroom slippers.

'You realise what this means?' Patrick said.

Liz stared at him. Then she understood.

'He's not on the Schneiderhorn. He couldn't have gone ski-ing without his boots. He must be somewhere in the village.'

'Right. All those men are wasting their time and risking their necks unnecessarily. I suppose the rest of your party were too British to think of poking about in here,' said Patrick grimly. 'He had another pair of shoes, presumably. Whatever he wore under his galoshes.'

'He had a pair of ordinary laced shoes, black ones. I never noticed the galoshes.'

Patrick closed the wardrobe and opened the drawer of the bed-side chest. In it were a packet of corn plasters, three foil-wrapped individual doses of Eno's salts, a bottle of Disprin and a packet of indigestion tablets.

'No letters. No photographs. No papers,' said Patrick. He lifted down Bernard's case from the top of the wardrobe and looked inside. It was empty. 'He must have carried his passport and all his money on him. A suspicious nature,' said Patrick. 'What a sad little room. What a drab little life. Why weren't his ski-boots put out for cleaning, I wonder? They do look clean. We would then have known he was not wearing them, for the maid would have noticed.'

'They do them early here, I mean at night, not in the morning. The maid who turns down the beds does them,' Liz said. 'He could have put them away before coming down to the disco-theque.' Something else struck her, and her heart sank. 'Of course, he can't have gone ski-ing. We should have known.' She told Patrick what the maid had said about Bernard's pyjamas.

'Dear, dear,' said Patrick. 'And even that didn't prompt anyone to see if his boots were here?' He shook his head sadly. 'Well, we must get those men down from the mountain without delay. I'll just make a quick note of these addresses.' He took out his wallet, extracted a small pocket diary from it, and scribbled down the names and addresses on the two postcards. Liz watched him in a stunned way.

'Why are you doing that?' she asked.

'We may find it useful to know them. Mrs. D. B. Walker in Woking, that will be his mother, and R. J. Fisher Esq., the Town

Clerk's Office, Wapshot. His colleague, perhaps. Right.' Patrick replaced the cards, put his wallet away, and turned to Liz. 'Come and vouch for me with Frau Scholler,' he said. 'That will be the quickest way to get the search switched from the mountain.'

It had to be done. Liz presented him formally to Frau Scholler as a lecturer from the University of Oxford and a guest of Professor Klocker. Patrick then said, with perfect truth, that since no one remembered seeing the missing man on the Schneiderhorn the day before he had wondered if in fact he had gone ski-ing after all, and so he had looked for the boots.

Frau Scholler did not seem to think him over-zealous. She was grateful.

'The men will be brought down,' she said, after speaking on the telephone. 'Thank you, Dr. Grant.'

'Now I'm going to make a telephone call,' Patrick said. 'But first, I'm going to look for the galoshes.'

And he left Liz gaping after him as he disappeared into the men's cloakroom.

## III

Penny, working on the maxim that the show must at all costs go on, decided to divert her clients with a fondue party that night at the Gentiana, instead of the normal dinner. She co-opted the party at the Silvretta, who, since none of them had met Bernard, were affected only in an academic sense by his disappearance. It was out of the question to plead another engagement; all were obliged to accept. By this time the village was being systematically searched for Bernard; the ski instructors, brought down from the mountain without calamity, were going from house to house inquiring for him, but since his passport was not available they had no photograph and their task was, as Sam had foreseen, difficult.

'He'll turn up, he's the sort of person nothing ever happens to,' said Sue. 'He could even be hiding on purpose to cause a stir.'

'Oh, nonsense,' Liz contradicted. 'He may be dim, but he's not as stupid as that.' They were in the Whittakers' room, where they had been invited for drinks before the fondue party together with Sam and the Derringtons; they were all drinking gin and mineral water out of toothmugs, and nibbling peanuts from paper packets.

'Where can he have gone after he left the discotheque?' Barbara asked. 'One would have expected him to go straight to bed. But obviously he didn't, from what the maid said.'

'You mean about his pyjamas? I suppose you're right.' It wouldn't be so bad if Bernard had disappeared on Sunday morning; his chances of survival would be much greater. No one could have survived outside during Saturday night when there was such a heavy snowfall.

'He was pretty embarrassingly involved with Fiona,' Sam said. 'Maybe he took her for a walk to cool down.'

'You mean he may have thought that safer than going with her back to the annexe?' Sue asked.

'I wouldn't pass up a chance to go back to the annexe with Fiona,' Freddie remarked.

'No, I bet you wouldn't,' said his wife.

Sam answered Sue: 'Yes. Or he may have wanted to give her time to get back, without the risk of running into her. I mean he may have hung about till he thought she'd gone.'

Liz had been over all this ground with Patrick already. He had found Bernard's galoshes in the cloakroom. *B. Walker* was written neatly in indelible ink inside them, as in a schoolboy's shoes. Patrick had left them where they were.

'Let's change the subject,' she said, shifting her position on the window sill so that she was not facing Francis. 'Going over all this isn't going to find Bernard.'

'Well, I for one wish we were having an ordinary dinner tonight,' Freddie declared. 'Fondue's all very well, but when you've had one, you've had them all. Give me a decent four-course meal every time.'

'We must make an effort for Penny's sake,' said Barbara. She seemed very shaken by Bernard's disappearance and had tossed down two strong drinks in the minimum time. 'Poor girl, she's so conscientious that she thinks keeping us busy is part of her job.'

'So it is,' said Hilda. 'But not all couriers are like her. Some get you out, more by luck than organisation, and just dump you, and you don't see them again till it's time to leave a fortnight later. Not that it matters to us, we just use the tour for cheap travel, but it's hard on people who don't know the ropes.'

'It must be a simply frightful job,' said Barbara. She was dressed in emerald green this evening, with her blonde hair piled high; several bracelets chinked on her wrist. 'I suppose these girls do it for an opportunity to travel.'

'Or for the men. They must meet plenty,' said Hilda.

'Maybe they just like ski-ing,' said Francis mildly.

'Fiona does all right, anyway,' Sue said. 'Her wounds seem pretty well healed.'

'What wounds?'

'She had some unhappy *affaire* – thought she was going to marry this chap and he chucked her for no reason. Penny persuaded her to come out here to get over it, and found this job for her. That's why she feels so responsible for her.'

'She certainly wasted no time in getting her hooks into Roy,' said Barbara. 'The classic rebound, probably.'

'Well, she might have rebounded in some other direction, not his,' said Liz. 'There must be plenty of unattached men in Greutz.'

'June was in tears this afternoon when Barbara and I went to see her, wasn't she, Barbara?' Sue looked at the other woman for confirmation, and Barbara nodded.

'Roy'd only been in for five minutes this morning,' she said.

'Perhaps he can't bear to see anyone ill,' said Sam. 'Some people are like that.'

'Maybe, but in sickness and health and all that, and she isn't ill, only battered,' Sue said roundly.

'Oh, I'm not excusing him, only trying to find a reason,' said Sam hastily. Sue was formidable when roused.

'Well, I'd rather have an armful of Fiona, however plastered, than the pale June, drunk or sober,' stated Freddie. He and Sam sat side by side on one of the beds, while Hilda and Sue occupied the only chairs in the room. 'We travelled out with them, remember. She was nervous on the flight and felt sick in the bus. Very much the old-fashioned pure English virgin. An odd match, isn't it? I'd have expected Foster to go for something a bit more mettlesome.' As he spoke, his eyes were on Barbara, stretched out on the other bed, slim and graceful.

Liz had been watching them all the while they talked; she felt so tense herself that it seemed to her the air was crackling. Now she noticed that Francis was looking at his wife with a speculative expression on his face. Barbara was a very attractive woman, Liz could see; she looked at Freddie once again, and then at Hilda, and in Hilda's eyes she saw mirrored her own thoughts. She was not imagining all the tensions she could sense; they were real.

She stood up.

'Let's go down,' she said. 'It's after eight. Penny will be afraid someone else is lost.'

The *stube* where the fondue was to be held was arranged with three round tables each set for eight people. Penny and her clients from the Silvretta were already there; the other group consisted of ten young people, none over thirty. Judging by the noise, they were all in party humour. Among them were Fiona and Roy. Standing a little apart, looking dignified despite their informal garments, were Patrick, Professor Klocker, and Jan.

'We are joining you. Penny invited us all,' said Patrick.

'Surprise, surprise. I might have known,' muttered Liz.

'Why? Aren't you pleased?' he asked her. 'I thought you needed me.'

She gave him a look.

'You know I'm pleased, dope,' she said. 'And just look at those two.' For Jan and Sue were already whispering together.

Penny took charge, getting everyone to the tables, and the waitresses came in with spirit stoves, setting them in position and adjusting the flames. Six people from the Silvretta, with Roy and Fiona, filled one table; the other four went to a second, where Penny clearly proposed to join them.

'We need three more here to make the table up,' she said. 'What about you and Jan, Sue? And Sam?'

It was arranged. Sue seated herself happily between the two men; Sam seemed content; he appeared to have surmounted the inhibitions he had earlier displayed; Liz thought he might just have been shy, there was no need to seek more deeply for the reasons. The rest of them took their places at the third table and she found herself with Francis on one side of her and Professor Klocker on the other. Patrick faced her, with Hilda on his right. Barbara was on the professor's other side, with Freddie next to her. There was one space left.

'God, they've laid for Bernard,' muttered Liz.

Francis, who was nearest, spoke to the waitress who removed the extra cover with blushes of apology.

'That's a good start to the evening,' he murmured to Liz.

Those at the other two tables had noticed nothing; they were busy inspecting the arrival of the dishes laden with spices and garnishes, and the huge platters of raw steak, neatly cubed. Soon the room was filled with a cheerful sizzling sound as the meat, spiked on long holders, began to cook in the boiling oil.

'I suppose this gives the staff a rest, putting the guests to work cooking their own food,' said Patrick, poking about in the cauldron for a hunk of beef that had come dislodged from his skewer.

'It's a racket,' Freddie said. 'Making us pay for this on top of our all-in terms, and vino too. Has anybody ordered it? No? I will, then.'

He summoned Else, and she went off, to return with two large carafes of the rough red local wine.

'We'll be sorry about this tomorrow, I feel already,' Liz said grimly, when she had downed one glass of wine and let Francis fill her glass again.

'You are a pessimistic person, Liz,' he said. 'You always fear the worst, don't you? Don't look so far ahead; we've got to get through the evening first.'

'It's going to be tough going,' Liz said.

'It needn't be,' he answered in a quiet voice. 'Just live for the moment.'

And the moment included him, beside her. Liz drank some more wine. It might help.

Hilda Derrington was talking to Max about the weather, across the pan of cooking meat which separated them.

'Surely it must improve soon?' she said.

'One would expect so, by the law of averages. But it is still very warm, and the glass is too low,' the professor replied. 'I'm afraid it doesn't look too good for tomorrow. But it can alter suddenly.'

'We were in Zermatt once when there was an avalanche that cut us off for several days. Everyone got so bad-tempered.'

'It's unpleasant, feeling that you can't get away,' said Max.

'It's such a waste of the holiday, too,' said Hilda. 'Especially when it's the only one you get.'

'You don't have a summer vacation, then? Many people seem to take two breaks in the year.'

'Not mink farmers. We're too broke, and we're busy in the summer with the kitts,' Hilda answered. 'Actually, Freddie had a week in Malta last summer, but that was because his uncle died out there and he had to clear things up. I was left at home literally holding the babies.'

'And a fine job you made of it, too,' said Freddie, overhearing. 'When I got back half of them had been eaten by their mothers.'

'That wasn't my fault,' Hilda protested.

'What a horrible thing to happen,' Barbara exclaimed, quite put off her *bourguignonne*. 'What made them do such a thing?'

'They're temperamental brutes. Any sudden noise, like an aircraft flying low over them, upsets them and can cause it,' Freddie said.

'Did something like that happen?'

'Yes. A fool friend of Hilda's came to visit her in a helicopter, if you please. Landed on the lawn.'

'Are you insured against that sort of thing?' Patrick inquired.

'It's not an act of God,' Freddie said. 'And we'd been breeding for a new mutation. All that was lost.'

'You were in Malta in the summer, too, weren't you, Mrs. Whittaker?' Patrick asked Barbara. 'I think you told me so the other evening when we were dancing.'

'Yes, I was,' Barbara agreed. She told the others, 'A school-friend of mine lives there. I visit her most years.'

'I'm surprised you didn't meet Freddie, in that case,' Hilda said. 'The place is so small, everyone seems to know everybody else.'

'How could I, unless we were both there at the same time?' Barbara replied smoothly.

As she spoke, the lights flickered. Then everyone heard it, a long, rumbling roar, like thunder or a prolonged explosion, that echoed on for what seemed like several minutes. The lights flickered again; then they went out.

Under the fondue pans the flames burned on with scarcely a waver and gave a dim light to the room. Everyone stopped talking when the noise began; then there was a sudden burst of excited speech as each began to wonder what had happened.

'Do not be afraid,' said Professor Klocker's calm voice. 'That was not close. There will be no danger here in Greutz.'

'It sounded as if it was just outside,' said Liz.

Hilda Derrington calmly speared another piece of meat in the gloom and began to cook it.

'The echo from the valley makes it sound near,' the professor said. 'That must have been at least a mile away.'

A buzz of talk had broken out now. Some of the young men at the other tables wanted to go outside and see what had happened, and Penny was pleading with them to stay where they were. Before many minutes had passed, Frau Scholler came bustling in bearing a candle, followed by Else and the other waitress who carried more candles stuck in bottles, which they put on the tables. She said that no one knew exactly where the avalanche had fallen, but it was certainly not in Greutz; it was somewhere towards Kramms, perhaps where the small fall had been a few days before. The telephone was working normally, so there would soon be more news, but the power supply had gone.

By the light of the candles the meal continued, though now with an undercurrent of unease. After a while Professor Klocker spoke to Patrick.

'I am a little concerned for Helga,' he said. 'I will go home, if you will all excuse me,' he added to the others. 'She will telephone me, if she can.'

'Of course, Max. I'll come too,' said Patrick, getting up.

'No, no, Patrick. You stay here and complete the evening. You can do nothing. But I would like to be where I can be reached.

I am too old to be of much real use if help is needed, but you are not. If there is no serious damage, you can bring me the news later.'

The professor made his farewells to everyone and left.

'At least we have a doctor in the village, if there are casualties. How awful to be just sitting here when perhaps people have been buried,' said Barbara.

'I suppose there is nothing we can do?' Patrick asked Francis.

'They've got their routine pretty well taped in these places,' Francis replied. 'If they want us, they'll say so. We'll only get in the way if we rush about trying to find out what's happened.'

At the middle table Jan was lamenting.

'Sue, with no electricity for the discotheque, how can we dance? No power, no music.'

'You can have your music,' Sam said.

In a corner of the room was an old upright piano. He crossed to it, opened it, and began to play dance music from the 'fifties. He played with verve, and at once Jan swept Sue out among the tables and they began to dance. Soon, more couples followed.

'What a man of parts Sam Irwin has turned out to be,' Patrick observed.

'Oh what a dreadful pun,' said Liz disgustedly.

'I didn't mean it as one. You're ticking over just a bit too fast, my love,' he told her reprovingly. He turned to Barbara. If Liz must after all play with fire he would let her have her chance by removing the obvious obstacle. Sedately circling round with Barbara, he had the dubious satisfaction of seeing Liz dance with Francis Whittaker in what he thought of as a pretty close clinch.

The Derringtons, left at the table, appeared to be arguing. The next time Patrick looked for them they had both disappeared.

Bernard seemed to have been successfully forgotten.

## PART FIVE

# Tuesday

## I

A SMALL boy on his way to school the next morning dropped a marble on the covered wooden bridge. It fell between two of the planks, and the little boy squatted down to see if he could find it. Eye to a slit in the wood, he saw something strange below in the black water. It was a human arm and a gloved hand. Bernard had been found.

The bridge was rapidly screened from curious eyes while the burgomeister supervised Bernard's removal from the river. He lay with one arm round a boulder, and his head floated, bobbing in the gentle eddy.

Patrick, standing on the professor's balcony, saw the activity below and hurried down in time to see the body lifted from the water and laid on a stretcher. Someone spread a blanket over it, and it was carried into the clinic, conveniently close. Patrick firmly followed it inside.

The burgomeister was only too thankful to have some compatriot of the dead man with whom to share the responsibility of this disaster, for he had enough on his mind already with the avalanche to think about. When Patrick, producing his passport, had demonstrated his own probity, he was allowed to look at Bernard, now lying on a scrubbed table in a bare room. He wondered if the clinic dealt with many fatalities, and thought it unlikely; there might be occasional climbing accidents, but cases of serious illness would be taken to a town.

'You will undertake to inform the relatives, Dr. Grant? That would be most kind. There must be an inquiry as to what has happened – a mere formality, you understand – Herr Walker slipped in some accidental manner into the river. But first we have to clear the damage from last night's snowfall, and get the roads open again.'

Patrick's German was quite good, and he had no difficulty in understanding the dilemma of the burgomeister. A small chalet had been swept away by the avalanche, burying four people; the road was blocked with an immense barrier of snow, uprooted trees and debris. Every spare man was at work clearing it away.

A coffin would be provided, plain pine. The relatives would doubtless wish the sad cargo sent home as soon as conditions allowed. The burgomeister deeply regretted that such a thing had happened, and in Greutz of all places. The autopsy, which the law demanded, would be held as soon as possible but Dr. Wesser was not the official pathologist for the area, and this would have to wait. In any case it would be merely a matter of form.

'See his shoes. Most unsuitable,' said the burgomeister.

Bernard wore his black laced shoes; they had leather soles and were, as the burgomeister said, most unsuitable for walking in the snow.

'Being a doctor, you will understand what must have been the cause of death. He missed his footing, fell into the river, and was drowned,' said the burgomeister.

Patrick did not point out that his doctorate was not in medicine. As long as he was not expected to heal the sick, such a misapprehension might be useful.

'May I take his papers into safe keeping?' he asked.

'Of course.' The burgomeister was grateful for any relief to his load of worries.

Patrick bent over the body. The sodden anorak was fastened to the chin, and on the front of the chest was a zipped pocket. Inside this was a stout leather wallet, large enough to hold a passport. Patrick removed it, scrutinised it briefly, and wrapped it in his own handkerchief. He looked at Bernard's face. Strands of hair were plastered to the forehead. There was a slight flush over the cheekbones and around the mouth. He tipped the head gently to one side; there was no rigor. Probing, his fingers felt a bump behind one ear. He peered intently at the nose and into the mouth, which gaped open, and looked at the hands, examining them closely. Then he straightened.

'Thank you,' he said to the burgomeister. 'I will go and tell the other English people what has happened, and make arrangements for notifying his family. Later I will come for the clothes he is wearing, if you will see to that. There may be other papers in his pockets.'

'Of course. I will give instructions that everything is to be put ready for you,' said the burgomeister, heartily thankful that the deceased was a solitary traveller, and had left no widow needing consolation.

When Patrick left the clinic he saw that the little cluster of people who had gathered while Bernard was being lifted from the river had dispersed; the children were now, presumably, in school, and most of the visitors would be having breakfast. Patrick turned left across the bridge and went off to the Gentiana. He went straight up to Liz and Sue's room, where the maid was making the beds. She looked startled when he entered, but he told her briskly that he was a friend of the English ladies who would be up shortly; then he went into the bathroom and locked the door. To keep the maid happy he turned on one of the taps. Next he took Bernard's wallet from his own pocket and carefully unwrapped it. He unfolded it and took the contents out, spreading them about on the window sill and the basin and round the edge of the bath. After that he pulled the plug for the maid's benefit, and opened the door.

The woman had finished the beds. She looked at Patrick doubtfully, but luckily Liz arrived at that moment.

'Patrick! What on earth are you doing here?' she exclaimed.

'Tell the maid I'm your chum,' said Patrick. 'I think she's worried about my intentions.'

'*Das herren ist mein freund, is gut,*' Liz managed laboriously. The maid nodded and smiled, gave them both a coy look, bobbed, and left them to it.

'What a linguist you are,' said Patrick. 'I should think she takes an even more dubious view of my intentions now. Good!'

Liz felt it was too early in the day for such talk.

'Why are you here? What's happened?' she demanded.

'Bernard's been found.'

'Oh!' Liz sat down abruptly on one of the beds. 'He's dead, of course.'

'I'm afraid so.' Patrick told her how the body had been discovered.

'How ghastly! What an awful experience for the child who found him,' Liz said.

'Pretty grim,' Patrick agreed.

'Oh, poor Bernard. Somehow I kept hoping he'd turn up. What happened? Did he go for a walk and fall into the river?'

'That's what the burgomeister thinks. I'm not convinced it's quite as straightforward as that,' said Patrick. 'Just come in here a minute.'

He beckoned her into the bathroom, and Liz, who had years ago given up being surprised because he never reacted to anything in the manner of most people, followed. She saw all Bernard's papers spread around.

'Have a look at them. Touch anything you like,' he invited.

Liz picked up Bernard's passport and opened it. It was eight years old, showing its owner plumper and with a thicker crop of wavy hair. Some of the ink had run and blurred the information. She looked at the leather wallet and turned it over. Among the papers strewn about were a page of ski-school tickets, a ski-lift pass, a book of traveller's cheques, a holiday insurance policy, an air ticket and meal vouchers for the return journey. There was also a crumpled wad of paper money.

Suddenly she got it.

'They're only very damp. They're not saturated. The wallet's pretty sodden, but the water hadn't soaked right through.'

'That's my girl,' said Patrick. He pondered. 'I wonder if we'd better show them to Sue too, or will you do?'

'Do for what?'

'Do for a witness.'

'I don't understand.'

Patrick decided.

'We won't involve Sue, she's infatuated with that Dutchman and so not in her right mind. Liz, concentrate on this. It may help you to keep your balance. Bernard didn't drown. If he'd been in the river since Saturday night these things would all have been so wet we couldn't handle them. He was wearing a thick, padded waterproof anorak, it's true, but such a prolonged immersion would have penetrated through it. Besides, there were other signs.'

'What signs?' Liz ignored Patrick's reference to her emotional state.

'His hands, and his mouth and nostrils. No washerwoman skin on his hands, and not a sign of foam round his nose or mouth. Without a post-mortem it isn't evidence, but it's enough for me. I was suspicious already.'

'Why?'

'The galoshes. A man with such a cautious nature that he carries all his papers around with him even when he's spending the evening in his own hotel would never voluntarily go down the street dangerously shod.'

'But he must have left his anorak about, with all this stuff in it – no, he didn't, now I think of it. That wallet of his was always with him, he put it on the table like a woman might her purse, or else he kept his anorak on. And on Saturday he put his wallet in his shirt pocket, it bulged in a most odd way and Fiona grumbled about it when she was using his chest as a pillow.'

'I'm pleased to see you're quite observant,' Patrick said.

'But what are you driving at? I still don't get it?'

'If he'd accidentally fallen into the river, say because he was drunk, which we know he wasn't because you all say he was moderate in his habits, he'd have drowned,' Patrick explained patiently. 'But there was a bruise on his head. He might have hit it as he fell, but I think someone slugged him and left him to die either of exposure or suffocation from being buried under the snow.'

'Oh Patrick, no! Who on earth would want to do that to poor Bernard? He was much too insignificant to have any enemies. No friends, I know, but no one hated him. Besides, he didn't know anyone here. You're letting your imagination run away with you.'

'Maybe I am. I hope you're right, but I don't think you are,' said Patrick. 'When Dr. Wesser gets back to the clinic – he's down at the avalanche, helping there, some people were buried – I'm going to ask him to look at the bump on Bernard's head. Meanwhile, the official view is that he drowned, and that's the one we must uphold. We must tell Robin Hood and the rest of your band.'

'What about his family? There was a mother, didn't you decide?' Liz picked up the passport again. 'Born in Newbury, in 1925. So he was as old as that, goodness. Occupation, civil servant. No address, of course.'

'There were addresses on those postcards,' Patrick reminded her. 'I hope to have some more information about him later on today. I rang up a friend of mine in England to ask him to do a bit of sleuthing for me, and I'm calling him later to see what he's unearthed.'

'Patrick! You mean you suspected something fishy before Bernard turned up? Or are you up to your usual tricks of stirring up trouble? You love disturbing hornet's nests.' Liz was looking at him in horror. 'One day you'll go too far, meddling in what isn't your business.'

'It's the duty of every citizen to uphold the law,' said Patrick austerely. 'And if one suspects foul play one must speak up, or seek the truth, or both. It was the galoshes that made me suspicious. If the poor fellow was clobbered, you want him avenged, I hope. I thought a few background details might be helpful, just in case the worst had happened. Best to sort this out discreetly if we can, before involving the authorities. They're much too busy at the moment, anyway.'

'But who could – you mean someone among us? I can't believe it. I won't believe it.'

'You say he was always scuttling about. Maybe he saw something he wasn't meant to?'

'You mean he was blackmailing someone?'

'He might have been.'

Liz at once remembered the glance that had passed between

Barbara Whittaker and Freddie Derrington the night before, and the tension she had felt between them. At least Patrick had not been present then, so that was something he did not know to add fuel to his fire. There was Roy, too, involved with Fiona, but that was no secret; its very blatancy was one of its most distasteful aspects. She shivered. 'No, I won't believe it. It's too outrageous,' she declared.

'We'll see,' said Patrick.

'You're not to go upsetting everybody.'

'I don't propose to. This is just between ourselves, until we have some proof,' Patrick said. 'Now, is there somewhere safe in here where we can put all these things of Bernard's?'

'There's my suitcase. It's empty except for my passport and traveller's cheques and so on. I keep it locked. They'd dry out safely in there, I suppose. But shouldn't you tell the police or whoever's in charge here what you've just told me?' If he did, and authority quickly proved him wrong, that would be the end of the matter.

'A short delay won't hurt. Our man – or woman – can't escape, and the burgomeister has his hands full coping with the avalanche. There's no policeman living in Greutz, they'd have to send in someone from outside, so it would be a stalemate anyway till the roads are cleared. Nothing will be lost, and much may be gained if I do some quiet research first. Besides, this is a British matter,' Patrick said. 'But we must tell the rest of your group he's been found. We must act very normally, Liz, and not let it seem that we think it's more than an accident. Don't give anything away, will you? And keep your eyes open for any odd happenings.'

Liz sighed.

'I suppose I must,' she said. 'You horrible man.'

## II

Sounds of music came from the *stube*, where Sam, spurred on by his success the evening before, was amusing himself at the piano.

Francis was in the room, too, sitting on the hard wooden window seat and reading an old *Reader's Digest.* Penny sat at a table balancing her accounts for the previous night's fondue party.

They listened in silence while Patrick told them about the discovery of Bernard's body.

'Well, I suppose we were expecting to hear something of this sort,' Francis said when he had finished. 'But it's a shocking thing, all the same. I'm sorry.'

'It's quite awful,' said Penny. 'I suppose I must tell London. And there will be things to do, arrangements and such-like.'

'I think you'd better let London know, yes. I told the burgomeister we'd see to that side of things,' agreed Patrick. 'But nothing else can be decided until the roads are cleared.'

'He must have some family,' Penny said. 'Everyone's got somebody. How on earth do we track them down?'

'Your London office will deal with all that,' Francis said. 'They'll get on to the police.'

'What on earth can he have been up to, wandering around in the night like that?'

'I don't suppose we'll ever know,' said Sam.

'Is there anything I can do?' Francis asked. 'There must be formalities.'

'There are, but they can't be dealt with until the avalanche has been cleared from the road and things are rather more sorted out,' said Patrick. 'The poor burgomeister has got his hands full. Where's everybody else?'

'The girls are in the lounge, I think. Derrington's out somewhere, and I don't know where young Foster is,' said Francis.

Melancholy notes from the piano followed Patrick and Liz as they went through the hall and entered the lounge. Here they found Sue and Barbara discussing cooking with Hilda, while Frau Hiller listened to their conversation, meanwhile knitting a vast beige sweater.

'You've got news,' said Barbara, seeing their faces.

Patrick told them. For a moment no one spoke; Frau Hiller knitted stolidly on and the others, even Hilda, looked stunned.

'What was he doing down by the river?' asked Sue.

'That's what everyone's wondering,' said Liz. 'It seems extraordinary.'

'He may have been clearing his head,' said Patrick. 'From all accounts he seems to have made quite a night of it.'

'It wasn't his fault,' Sue said. 'It was Fiona who was being so embarrassing.'

'Well, thank goodness we know the answer now,' said Barbara. 'It would have been horrible to have gone home next weekend with him still missing.'

'That's true,' said Sue. 'Poor old Bernard. What an awful business.'

Penny came in then, having allowed Patrick time to break the news.

'I'm just going to ring up London,' she said. 'Isn't it dreadful? Maybe the priest would have a service for him. I don't know what we should try to arrange. There's no English church here.' She looked at Patrick for approval.

'That's an idea,' he said. 'Shall I mention it to the burgomeister? I'm going back to see him now.'

'Oh do. See what he thinks,' said Penny. 'Will you find out if he wants me to go and see him? I suppose I should. I'm responsible really.'

'He's a bit busy just now. Come down later when you've talked to London and perhaps got some response about his family,' suggested Patrick, who did not want the well-intentioned Penny getting in the way of his own researches.

'All right,' she agreed.

'Well, I'm off, then,' Patrick said.

He hurried away, head thrust forward, his fine dark hair flopping over his forehead, in just the manner in which Liz had so often seen him striding about Oxford in his gown, hurrying towards his next lecture. She was brought abruptly back to the present by Hilda.

'Your friend seems to have taken total charge of this affair,' she said in a petulant voice.

'Thank goodness,' said Penny fervently. 'You expect broken legs on ski-ing holidays, but not anything like this. I wish he'd ring up my London office for me, but I suppose that wouldn't be right. I'd better go and get on with it.'

She left them.

Frau Hiller rolled up her knitting, ran the needles through the ball of thick wool in a firm manner, and rose.

'Please excuse me if I leave you,' she said. 'I am so sorry about this sad affair. You will all want to talk,' and she walked away, rather flat-footed, her sweater rucked up round her waist revealing her plump back view in her black trousers.

'How sweet,' exclaimed Sue. 'She's being tactful. Now that I find rather endearing.'

Liz had been wondering wildly if Frau Hiller could be the murderer: she had stabbed her wool so fiercely; she was brawnily built; but what possible grudge could she bear against the unfortunate Bernard? Or had he been, perhaps, the victim of moon madness? How comforting if the villain were some maniac and not a sober citizen holidaying with Hickson.

'I must find Freddie,' Hilda declared. 'Goodness knows where he is.' She too went away.

'What an odd coincidence that your friend Dr Grant should be here,' Barbara said to Liz. 'Did you really not know he was coming? You seem to be such good friends.'

'We've known one another for years, but we don't meet very often,' Liz answered repressively.

'He doesn't seem to mind being stuck here,' Barbara observed, undeterred by Liz's cool tone.

'He's very philosophical,' Liz told her. 'He doesn't believe in unnecessary emotion.' But he noticed and understood it in others. 'I've got some mending to do,' she said. 'I'll go and get on with it.'

But instead of going up to her room, Liz found herself outside the hotel, heading towards the annexe. She was aware of no conscious plan, only some urge that compelled her without reason. She was wearing light pumps, even less suited to walking in the snow than Bernard's shoes, and she had no coat, but the snow had almost stopped; only an occasional flake was now spiralling down. A trail of many footmarks led across to the annexe, and like Wenceslas's page she trod in them. She went into the annexe and up the stairs. On the first landing, Bernard's door was closed and the key hung above it as Patrick had left it. Presumably it would be Penny's melancholy task to pack up his belongings. Liz went on, up the stairs to the next landing. Penny's room faced her; she knew which it was for she had been here for coffee one evening the week before, an age ago as it seemed now. Penny had a kettle and supplies in her room for private entertaining.

As she stood on the landing, hesitating, unable to account even to herself for why she had come, Liz heard voices. They came from Fiona's room, next to Penny's.

'They're sure to ask me. What shall I say?' This was Fiona speaking.

'They won't. It was an accident. They'll wrap it up in five minutes, there's nothing to worry about.' The second voice was Roy's.

'For God's sake give me a drink. There's some gin in the cupboard.' Fiona's voice was slurred.

'You've had enough. Pull yourself together. We've got to keep our heads,' Roy said. 'No one need know a thing. All we have to do is keep quiet and act normally. And I'll have to do my stuff with June.'

Gin at ten in the morning! And what did they want to hide? And how did they know so soon about Bernard? Neither was present when Patrick broke the news. Roy could have been to the clinic already and so discovered what had happened. A possible interpretation of what she had just heard came to her, and her heart began to pound uncomfortably. She turned away and went down the stairs again as quietly as she had come, crossed back to the main hotel and went up to her room.

There was no sign of Sue. Her anorak had gone from its hook behind the door, so presumably she was out, probably prowling round looking for Jan. A few minutes of the Dutchman's cheerful, uncomplicated company would be very refreshing just now, Liz thought. He, at least, was normal, healthily enjoying what was really a harmless flirtation which he would forget when it was over, though Sue would be sure to mope till she embarked on another. But not everyone in Greutz was so sanguine, alas, and as for herself, her own state was best not explored. Patrick was right: better to think about Bernard.

She took her own anorak down from the door. It was not a new one, but neither was Bernard's. It was still totally waterproof as a garment. She tore a thick wad from the old *Figaro* she had bought a few days before and put it into a pocket of her anorak, zipping it tightly. Then she ran some water into the washbasin in the bathroom and submerged the pocket and its surrounding area, festooning the sleeves and the rest of the anorak round the shelf and taps so that the whole thing did not get soaked. She wanted to prove Patrick's point for herself.

## III

When he left the Gentiana, Patrick, contrary to his expressed intentions, turned right at the end of the lane and took the road to Kramms. He remembered it from his drive with Max on Saturday, when they had visited an old man who had once been a celebrated pianist but who was now crippled with arthritis and spent his days in retirement among the mountains dreaming of the past during the winter, and in summer studying the flowers. The road ran along beside the river for a while, then climbed towards the col over the Wolfberg, a much smaller mountain than the Schneiderhorn but the source of a stream which lower down became the river flowing through Greutz. The avalanche had poured down the side of the Wolfberg forming a barrier many metres wide; it had swept into a new chalet, where the four people had been buried, but it had missed the older buildings which were sited well away from likely danger spots and well protected by trees above them.

Patrick met no one as he walked along; he came to the barrier with its warning notice where Liz had stopped, and passed beyond it, hoping not to encounter some minion of the burgomeister. The snow was very deep here, but a few tracks through it showed where the rescuers going down to the scene of the avalanche had driven. The road looped round to the left quite soon, hugging the river; on either side towered massive banks of snow piled up by the ploughs, but after going a short way Patrick came to a cutting between these banks on the river side; here the snow was not so deep, and clearly until the last day or so a path had been kept open at this point.

He turned down it.

It was hard going through such deep, soft snow, which came well up his thighs as he floundered along leaving considerable evidence of his passage; at least very little more was at present falling from the sky, which was some relief. But he had not far to go for the pathway ended abruptly at the river's edge, and the reason for the clearing was now made plain; there was a narrow footbridge over the river at this point and on the far side, among the trees, was a chalet.

Patrick did not step on to the bridge. He took off his glasses and cleaned them. Then he moved carefully along the downstream side of the bridge, treading cautiously as he sought for footholds along the bank. He went only a yard or two along the river's edge. He saw the branch of a tree caught against a boulder in the middle of the river; as he watched it was swept free, ran on a little way and then was held up again. More boughs and twigs could be seen in the water, and suddenly a lump of snow broke away from the bank and fell in. Patrick stood still, examining the ground near his feet and looking into the clear water which seemed so black under the lowering sky and surrounded by the brilliant whiteness of the snow.

He saw them there, caught against a stone below the surface: Bernard's spectacles.

Patrick left them where they lay. He turned back and gingerly made his way to firmer ground. No one saw him emerge from the forbidden area, and very soon he was back in the main thoroughfare of the village. He went straight to the Silvretta hotel, where there was a comfortable telephone cubicle affording privacy to its user, and put through a call to England. Next, he went to the burgomeister's office where he spent a very short time, and then he visited the clinic. He left there some time later carrying two parcels wrapped in brown paper. With one tucked under either arm, he walked back to the Gentiana.

Liz was standing in the hall looking at a framed map of the area which hung on the wall. On it, all the surrounding peaks could be distinguished : the Schneiderhorn stood out, round and massive, and to the east of it the smaller Wolfberg, and the neighbouring masses.

'Ah, Liz, there you are, good. Come back with me to lunch,' Patrick greeted her. 'I want to talk to you, but I promised to cook the lunch so that Max can get on with his book.'

'All right,' Liz agreed. 'I've certainly had enough of this place. We're all getting edgy, except for Sam who mellows hourly, and Sue who can think of nothing but Jan.'

'Let's hope our villain's nerves are among the jangled ones, even if it doesn't show,' said Patrick.

'You really believe it?'

'I really do.'

'Come upstairs,' she said.

'Oh, Liz, this is so sudden,' he replied, grinning.

'Fool. I want you for something,' she told him.

'Better and better.'

'There's a time and a place. Your levity is tasteless,' Liz said acidly.

'Good, good. I see you're recovering,' Patrick approved warmly.

She glared at him, but said no more, simply leading the way, and he followed, hearing the dry old boards creaking under his footsteps. In the bedrom he saw a candle in a bottle, ready for use later in case the power should still be off; the risk of fire, with ill-balanced candles stuck in bottles in this old, timber building made him shudder.

Liz went straight through the bedroom into the bathroom.

'Come in here,' she instructed.

He obeyed, and saw her anorak draped around the basin.

'What on earth – you didn't believe me!'

'I wanted to prove it.'

She let the water out of the basin and unzipped her anorak pocket. The newspaper within was a soggy, disintegrating mess. She consulted her watch.

'Almost two hours,' she said.

'Satisfied, Dr Watson?'

'Bernard's wallet was pretty thick. It was very wet. The leather would protect the other things to some extent, for a time, but it can't have been in the water long. Certainly not overnight. You must be right about that,' she admitted.

'I think he was in a snowdrift near the river bank. The vibration from the avalanche shook his bit of snow loose until eventually, but not for hours, it broke off and he fell into the water. He was washed down to the bridge, bumping a little from boulder to boulder which bruised his body – it is bruised, I've been looking at it – just before he was found, in my view,' said Patrick. 'The river is full of twigs and rubble which the avalanche brought down; they're all moving along downstream.'

'And he bumped his head, too, on the way?'

'Not necessarily. We need the doctor to say if he suffered that before or after death,' said Patrick. 'I think he was struck on the head and left in the snow. At the rate it was falling on Saturday night his attacker would know he would soon be buried and would die from suffocation or exposure, or both.'

'But, Patrick, if you're right, it's the most terrible, callous thing and someone should be trying to discover who did it,' Liz cried.

'I am trying to discover who did it,' said Patrick grandly.

'I don't mean you. I mean the police.'

'They can't, until a helicopter can get in. There isn't a copper in Greutz, it's administered from outside. And the powers-that-be won't like it anyway. They'd much rather it was an accident – bad for the carefree holiday image.'

'But justice would have to be done.'

'It will be anyway,' said Patrick grimly. 'I shall see to it.'

'Can't a helicopter come in now? It seems colder to me, and it's almost stopped snowing.'

'No. There are huge masses of snow piled up on the mountain tops just waiting for a bit of turbulence to bring them down. The burgomeister told me it will have to get much colder to fix the snow before they can come in,' said Patrick. 'But meanwhile our man or woman will have had a severe shock. He – we'll assume it was a man for argument's sake, but it could as easily have been a woman – will have expected Bernard to be lost without trace indefinitely, till the thaw, so he'll be putting on a big act now. With luck he'll make a slip and give himself away. Now, come along, Liz. I've got one little job you can help me with before you cook the lunch. What are you going to wear, to keep warm on the way, since you've sacrificed your anorak in the interests of forensic science?'

'I've got a coat,' said Liz. She hung her anorak over the towel rail in the bathroom and put the bathmat under it to catch the worst of the drips, and took the sheepskin coat she had travelled out in from the cupboard. She put it on, and her warm ankle boots, and tied a scarf over her head.

'What's the job, besides cooking the lunch? If ever there was a back-handed invitation – '

Patrick broke in.

'You brought June Foster's skis back from the clinic, didn't you? Would you know them again? Are they still here or have they been handed in?'

'As far as I know they're still here. I should think everyone's forgotten about them, I certainly had,' Liz said. 'Yes, I think I'd know them. I remember where I put them.'

'Thank goodness for an orderly female with a trained mind,' said Patrick. He set down one of his parcels. 'These are Bernard's clothes. They're dry but grubby. I'll leave them here for now. There was nothing interesting in his other pockets, just some coins and his front-door key.'

'Oh dear, must you?' Liz eyed the parcel in a resigned way.

'There's no point in carting it up to Max's. It'll have to be packed up with the rest of his things, after all. You'll probably end up in charge of the sad suitcase, if you aren't careful.'

Liz, warned, resolved that she would dodge this duty. Francis should undertake it. But Francis might be – no, she would not admit such a thought. How could Francis have any grudge against

Bernard? There were limits to how far she would follow Patrick with his theories, and some people must be absolutely free of all suspicion. Unbidden, the thought of Freddie Derrington and Barbara sprang into her mind, but could they be linked with Bernard?

'There was no little book?' she asked. 'No blackmailer's diary, full of scandal?'

'No. But the murderer would have taken it away, out of Bernard's pocket, if there had been,' said Patrick.

'What's in that other parcel?'

'June's ski-boots. Come along.'

Patrick led the way through the hall, past the dining-room and down to the ski-room by the indoor route. Then he undid the parcel. One of the boots had been cut to get it off June's foot on the injured leg; the other was intact.

'Now, which are her skis?'

The racks were full, for no one was out today, but Liz, with very little hesitation, lifted out a pair.

'I know these are hers, I put them in next to mine, and I noticed the number on them,' she said.

Patrick took them from her, undid them, and laid them on the ground. Then he pushed forward the levers which closed the clips over the toes of the boots, and placed the boots in position. He was able to fasten the undamaged one without much effort, but the damaged one needed considerable force.

Liz watched him.

'Well?' he said to her.

'Patrick, for God's sake, I'm not one of your wretched pupils, tell me what you're driving at,' she said.

'Isn't it obvious? One of the bindings was much too tight. If she fell, her ski wouldn't come off and if she fell in an awkward place there would be a good chance of her getting hurt. As she was a total beginner she was certain to fall eventually, particularly if she got too tired.'

Liz stared.

'You mean Roy – you mean he wanted her to break her leg? But they'd only just got married.'

'I suppose that isn't really what it sounds like, the *non-sequitur* to beat all,' said Patrick. 'He may not have intended her to hurt herself as badly as she did – a sprain or wrench might have been enough." He unfastened the boots, lashed the skis together and gave them to Liz to replace in a spot where she could find them again.

'I was afraid he might have adjusted the binding again by this time. He will, I expect. That will prove his guilt,' he said.

'But I don't understand,' Liz said. 'Couldn't it have been just a bad bit of fitting by the shop?'

'I know they're not always marvellous about adjusting skis in sportshops, but they make them fit so that you can do them up, and thereafter it's up to the wearer,' said Patrick. 'Roy could have screwed that clip up when June had got it on, she wouldn't have known any better, and no one else would have thought of looking at it. A *lehrer* might have, but they had no *lehrer* with them.'

'Well, I still don't see why he should want to do such a thing,' Liz insisted.

'Neither do I, yet. But I'm going to understand it all soon,' Patrick promised. 'Pop these boots up to your room with the rest of the stuff, will you, old girl? I'll wait here for you.'

It was a waste of breath to protest. Liz silently took the boots from him, carried them up to her room, locked them into her suitcase with Bernard's papers, since they seemed to be some sort of evidence, and returned to him. He was standing in the ski-room, staring round at the heaps of stacked skis and the stored toboggans, as if his mind were totally blank. They left together by the door that led to the lane.

As they walked through the village Liz told him about her excursion to the annexe.

'I don't know why I did it, or what I meant to do, in fact,' she said. 'I seem to have caught the prying habit from you. I never used to listen at doors.'

'Liz Morris, I'm proud of you,' he said. 'Do you suppose they're both still in there?'

'I don't know. I haven't seen either of them.'

'Maybe he wanted his little wife out of the way because Fiona seemed more exciting,' Patrick mused.

'Oh, Patrick, no! When he'd only just got married!'

'I wonder what the background is to that marriage. It seems a most unpromising alliance, doomed already. Do you think you could find out?'

Liz sighed a little.

'Sue already has. You know how soft-hearted she is. In the intervals of carrying on with Jan – I suppose they must come up for air sometimes – she's been having tea and sympathy with June. Roy's hardly been near her since the accident. It seems her father's a tycoon of some sort, very rich. She's an only child. Her mother and Roy's were at school together, the kids saw a lot of one another through the years and apparently drifted into the marriage. Roy farms somewhere in the Cotswolds. His father's dead and his mother's moving into a small house nearby, part of his farm. June loves riding and country life and she's a *Cordon Bleu* cook.'

'Hm. Miss Moneybags, eh?'

'Sounds like it.'

'Noticed anything funny about any of the others?'

'Not really. That is – ' Liz hesitated.

'What? Tell uncle. Is it about your Francis?'

'He's not my Francis,' said Liz furiously. 'And it isn't him, it's his wife. It's nothing really, and yet – I don't know.'

'Well, come on, then. Tell me.'

'It's Barbara and Freddie Derrington. They haven't met before, at least they haven't said so; and if they have they're superb actors, they carried it off marvellously on Saturday night. But there is something between them, I can sense it. And they were both in Malta last summer.'

'I remember them chatting about Malta. There was something odd about that conversation, I agree, but I don't know what exactly. They didn't start any of that "Did you meet old Joe?" stuff, seeking for mutual chums which one usually does on these occasions.'

'No, they didn't. And I thought Barbara definitely didn't want to pursue it.'

'It could be just coincidence. However, I'm a staunch believer in intuition, providing one can use it to discover facts,' Patrick said. 'What do you know about friend Francis that I don't?'

'Very little. You were there when he said he'd been married before. He told me he'd been a prisoner during the war and I told you. He hid somewhere near here after he escaped, I don't know where exactly. But none of us had met Bernard before.'

'It may not be anything like that. Bernard may have stumbled on something here in Greutz.'

'You mean he might have seen Roy fixing June's skis?'

'Not that. I doubt if anyone would have noticed that if Roy did it when June put them on. But some such thing, yes. Some shady business going on here under our noses.'

'Oh dear,' said Liz. 'I do wish I could prove that you're wrong, but I'm beginning to feel there is something in this idea of yours.'

'Well, bend your intellect towards helping me to discover what it is,' Patrick urged.

The priest came out of the little church as they went past it. He said to them, '*Gruss Gott*,' and walked on, hands thrust into the wide sleeves of his brown cassock, his woolly cap on his head and his beard curling on to his chest.

'Could it be a local thing?' Liz suggested desperately. 'Could Bernard have stumbled on some village feud? He spoke no German, or hardly any, but no one would know that.'

'Maybe,' Patrick conceded. 'It could be something like that, but if so I doubt if we'll ever get to the bottom of it.'

'Seeing the priest gave me the idea,' Liz said, relieved that Patrick had not instantly shot it down in flames. 'He's quite old. He must have been here during the war. Something may have happened then that they don't want to be reminded about.'

'I should think plenty of things did,' said Patrick thoughtfully. 'I get your point.'

The snow was much deeper on the road to the professor's chalet than in the main street, for fewer people had passed this way, but most householders had made some attempt at clearing it from their own pathways.

'It doesn't look as if Max will ever get his car out again,' said Patrick. 'And I'll be here for days.' Against the professor's garage door huge drifts of snow had collected. A narrow track led from the road to the front door. Patrick said he had cleared it before breakfast, but though the snow had slackened off during the morning it was coming down harder again now, in tiny stinging flakes.

'It's much colder,' Liz said. The glass has gone up, too. Did you notice?'

Patrick had. He inhaled deeply, standing on the front doorstep. Their twin tracks were sharply outlined in the soft new snow on the path behind them.

'The wind has changed direction,' he said. 'Perhaps an anti-cyclone's on its way.' He opened the door and they went in. Patrick took off his boots and anorak and put them in the cloak-room which led off the hall. 'Put your things in here, Liz,' he said. 'I'll tell Max you've come.'

Liz brushed her boots so hard that she could keep them on without risk of polluting Helga's polished floor. It was such a relief to walk around in ordinary sheepskin boots instead of heavy, unyielding ski-boots. Patrick went through to the study. The professor was sitting at his desk, papers spread all round him.

'Ah, Patrick, is it snowing again?' he asked.

'Yes, but not hard. Had a nice, peaceful morning? I've brought Liz back to cook the lunch. Pork chops, I took them from your freezer earlier.'

'Splendid. What time is it?'

'It's just after twelve.'

'Good gracious, is it? I thought it was only about eleven o'clock.' The professor gathered together a sheaf of papers. 'I've just been amending those footnotes in the final chapter. Have you had a satisfactory morning?'

'It depends how you define satisfaction,' Patrick said. 'The missing skier has been found.'

'Oh?' The professor looked at Patrick over the top of his glasses and then said 'Oh' again on a different note. 'I see by your face that the news is not good,' he said. 'Where was he?'

'In the river. He'd been washed down to the bridge.' Once again Patrick described how the body had been found.

'How very sad,' said the professor. 'I'm so sorry. What a tragedy.'

'I'll leave you to wind up your chapter and tell you the rest at lunch,' said Patrick.

'Yes, indeed,' the professor agreed. 'Do that. Poor man. Ah well.' He picked up his pen, half his attention still with his sources.

Patrick found Liz already in the kitchen peeling potatoes. She wore a large yellow apron she had found on a hook behind the door. It was big enough to go round her twice.

'You look quite enchanting,' Patrick told her. He got the rum from the cupboard and poured out two tots. 'You can knock off drink when you get home,' he said. 'You need it now to keep you going through this *crise*. Now then, while you cook, I'll cogitate.'

'Do it aloud, please.'

'All right.' Patrick raised his glass. 'To justice,' he said, swallowed half its contents, and began.

'We have here a group of British holiday-makers, as far as we know none of whom had met before except for those who came in couples, namely the Whittakers, the Derringtons, the Fosters, and you and Sue.'

'I hope you're not casting us in the role of suspects?'

'Not at present. Sue's been far too busy.'

'Jan – ' Liz hesitated.

'Well?'

'No. Nothing. Jan couldn't possibly have anything to do with it. And he hasn't tried to hide his frolic with Sue, so that's no motive, though he is married.'

'I imagine the frolic, as you so charmingly describe it, is pretty harmless,' Patrick observed dryly.

'I refuse to give an opinion.'

'Don't be so prim. But it's possible that if some local feud were involved, as you suggested, connected with the war, there could be a link with Jan.'

'Not very likely, is it? We're a long way from Holland, and he's too young.'

'I agree it's far-fetched, but he must have had a father, brothers possibly – relations who could have been deported. And physically he's very strong; he could easily have carried Bernard's body before dumping it.'

'Don't you think he was killed down by the river?'

'Not really. From the impression I have of his character I think it unlikely that he would have walked there voluntarily, and particularly without his galoshes. Anyway, to return to our list, in addition to our three British couples and you two, we have Fiona, a sexy piece if you like them angular and pixilated; Penny, who is adorable; Sam Irwin, who is complicated; and Bernard. They were all together that night when Bernard was last seen alive.'

'Surely it must have been the Derringtons or the Fosters?' said Liz.

'Why do you say that?'

'Because he disappeared as soon as they arrived. If it was anyone else, they'd have done it sooner.'

'Not necessarily. You say he was always scuttling about. If he was a sort of peeping Tom and petty blackmailer it may have taken him a week to find out something he could act on.'

The chops were sizzling nicely now, and Liz was making a sauce to pour over them before finishing them in the oven.

'Smells good,' said Patrick. 'You're wasted in single life.'

Liz ignored this.

'I don't see how you can possibly find out any more. It's all just theory,' she said. 'Maybe he did have a scuffle with someone he was spying on, but they can't have meant to kill him.'

'I do know some more,' Patrick informed her. 'I had an interesting telephone conversation this morning with Colin Smithers. You know who I mean.'

'That's your copper pal, isn't it? He's at Scotland Yard now, you said.'

'The same. And he's been promoted, too. He's a Detective Inspector now. I asked him to check what he could from the addresses on those postcards Bernard had written, and what I knew about everyone else.'

'Patrick! You mean you got him ferreting about into the affairs of all of us? The Whittakers and the Derringtons? You go too far.'

'Oh, it was all done very discreetly. He hasn't had time to turn up much so far, but now we know Bernard's dead there really is something to investigate. He was very interested in what I told him this morning.'

'Well, I suppose I'd better hear the worst,' Liz said. She put the chops into a fireproof dish and poured the sauce over them.

'Colin has a good contact in the Cotswolds,' Patrick went on. 'I say, what a sentence.'

'Patrick has pretty peculiar pals,' Liz retorted tartly. 'Fifteen love.'

'Sorry. Where was I?'

'In Bourton-on-the-Water, Stow-on-the-Wold, or somewhere. But you didn't know the Fosters lived there, I told you that this morning. How did he find out?'

'He didn't. I did know, because I discovered it by inquiring down at the clinic before I rang Colin up yesterday. But naturally I couldn't ask about the marital background; your information on that was most valuable, Liz.'

'You asked me for it,' she said coldly.

'Well, to proceed: it seems Roy Foster's farm is mortgaged to the hilt. It's been in the family for generations, yeoman farmer stuff I think originally, but Roy's a bit of a good-time lad and has frittered away his assets. Wedding astonished all the locals – June's father to the rescue, one would surmise.'

'What a silly girl,' Liz shuddered. 'Nowadays, one would think she'd have more sense.'

'Moonlight plays tricks, you know,' Patrick said lightly. 'Where was I?'

'Casting doubts on everyone.'

'Ah yes. The Derringtons, now. I couldn't give Colin anything to start from about them, but they talked about their mink losses last night so we know they're in some financial trouble.'

'Not enough to prevent them having a holiday. Pity you can't prove it was Bernard in the helicopter visiting Hilda and frightening the mink,' Liz said sarcastically.

'Even Bernard may have had his hour of glory once,' said Patrick mildly.

'What did your policeman friend have to say about him?'

'He wasn't the town clerk of Wapshot, as he'd implied. He was just a clerk in the municipal offices. He lived in a bed-sitter in the borough and attended evening classes in woodwork. He was a dutiful son and went home every weekend to his mother who is a sprightly old lady involved with townswomen's guilds, Derby and Joan clubs and the like. A dominant figure, in fact. He had no girl-friends, and no hobbies apart from carpentry. He didn't even run a car. He was in the R.A.S.C. for the last two years of the war and rose to the dizzy rank of corporal, and he served in Holland after the D-Day landings.'

'Holland!' Liz said, and then quickly, 'But Jan was a child.'

'Yes,' said Patrick. 'Putting sand into petrol tanks. He told us so.'

At this point Max joined them.

'There is a most delicious smell coming from here. You have enticed me away from my work, Mrs. Morris,' he said, and added, looking at their grave faces, 'I suppose you are discussing this sad business about your countryman.'

'Yes. Patrick's full of wild ideas about it.'

'Is he? Tell me what they are.' The professor topped up their glasses and poured himself out a tot from the rum bottle. 'Surely it was an accident? He had too much to drink, perhaps, and fell into the river?'

'No, Max. It isn't as simple as that. The body hadn't been in the water long. It lacked the typical features of death by drowning – froth in the throat and nose, wrinkled skin on the hands and feet. Without a post mortem one can't be sure, of course, but Dr Wesser agrees that I may be right. I saw him when he got back from the scene of the avalanche this morning, quite some time after Bernard was brought in.'

'There will have to be a post-mortem, anyway,' said the professor.

'Yes, but I understand the pathologist lives over in the next valley. Bernard will have to be removed for it. I suppose Wesser may be ordered to do it if there's a prolonged delay.'

'There's no refrigeration at the clinic,' said the professor.

'Exactly,' said Patrick grimly.

'What do you mean – oh, how horrible,' Liz exclaimed.

'Quite,' said Patrick. 'Fiona, as far as we know, was the last person to see Bernard alive,' he went on. 'She's elusive, isn't she? I must talk to her.'

'Find Roy and you'll find Fiona,' Liz said. 'Maybe he took a shine to her straight away, on Saturday, and he and Bernard had a fight over her. Roy would have had no qualms about leaving Bernard lying in the snow. Did Colin know anything about her?'

'He hasn't got that far. He's on to it now,' said Patrick.

'Well, I'm glad someone's private life is still their own,' said Liz. She turned to the professor, who had been looking somewhat bewildered during this exchange. 'I don't know how you got mixed up with Patrick, Professor, but he's a beastly man. He won't ever leave things be. He's sure someone killed Bernard.'

'But why should anyone want to do that? From what you've said about him it sounds as if he was a harmless, ineffectual sort of person.'

'Exactly. He was just that. Dreadfully dull, and he behaved mysteriously to make himself seem more interesting,' Liz said firmly.

'He acted out of character in going for a walk without his galoshes,' Patrick said. 'If he wore them just to cross from the annexe to the main hotel, he'd certainly put them on to go back again; and if he left the Gentiana with the intention of going for a walk, all the more reason to wear them.'

'Maybe Fiona was so impatient she wouldn't let him go and fetch them,' Liz suggested.

'Now who's being fanciful? Can you imagine Fiona really wanting to tangle with Bernard?'

'Fiona is the young woman who operates the record-player?' asked the professor.

'That's right.'

'She might for want of something better, or to make someone jealous,' Liz declared. 'She could have killed him, too. Why are we so sure it was a man?'

'We aren't, if he was lured to where he was killed. But a woman couldn't have carried him.'

'Some women could have,' Liz said slowly. 'He was slim and can't have weighed much. Hilda's pretty beefy. But she'd have had no motive. Suppose it was Fiona, and it was just an accident? She and Bernard went down to the river amorously entwined, Bernard having passed up the galoshes in the excitement. He lost his balance and fell over – that's possible – and she was bored because he obviously wasn't in her league, so she left him there, thinking he'd soon get up again, and went off herself. Then she got scared when he was missing and that's why she and Roy were in a worried huddle this morning. That must be it.' Liz was pleased with this theory. 'It holds,' she said.

'Yes, it does,' Patrick conceded.

'And it was an accident, as I've said all along.'

'We agree that the general opinion is that Bernard wasn't drunk that night?'

'No, he wasn't. There's no doubt about that.'

'Then I don't see him going for this famous walk with Fiona. From what you say he was scared of women – probably led a rich fantasy life, wild in the extreme, but faced with real opportunity would run as fast as he could in the opposite direction.'

'I have to admit that I don't understand why Fiona picked on him that night,' Liz admitted. 'There were plenty of chaps in the nightclub that night who were far better prospects. He was scarcely the answer to a randy girl's prayer.'

'Liz! Your language!' Patrick exclaimed, his eyes almost vanishing behind his thick-framed glasses as he burst into laughter.

The professor was smiling, too.

'You are a most refreshing person, if I may say so, Mrs Morris,' he told her. 'You certainly don't mince matters.'

'Please call me Liz, Professor,' she asked. 'Patrick!'

'Well?'

'You haven't mentioned Francis.' She looked at him steadily. 'Did your pal find out anything about his grisly past?' She turned to the professor and explained, 'Patrick has some policeman friend in London he's been asking for information about us all.'

'No. He simply confirmed that the caravan encampment is tastefully managed, and the Whittakers are respected in the district. We knew already that Francis was in this area during the war.'

'He needn't have told us. He volunteered it himself. If he'd anything to hide, he'd have kept quiet.'

'One would imagine so, yes.'

'What about Sam?'

'Ah yes, poor Sam. Now he's been a bit unlucky. A few years ago he went to a party where there was a raid. Drugs were found, and he was fined. Afterwards he had a breakdown and was in hospital for some time. That was why he couldn't fulfil his contract. Colin seemed to think the general feeling was that he'd been framed – professional jealousy, possibly, or jealousy of some other sort. But anyway, he bought it.'

'Poor Sam. I see. But it doesn't connect up with Bernard.'

'I agree, unless by some odd chance he was also at the drug party, but that's rather a fanciful idea.' Patrick pondered. 'Sue's Dutchman was around on Saturday night, wasn't he? Or had he gone back to his own hotel before Bernard went into the gloaming with Fiona, assuming that he did?'

Liz wondered whether to tell Patrick about the figure she had seen in the corridor that night. Not yet, she decided.

'I don't think he had. Sue was quite late coming to bed. She'd been spooning somewhere or other,' she said.

'What a delightful old-fashioned expression, "spooning".' Patrick rolled it round his tongue. 'I love your use of language, Liz. I must get you to give a lecture to my nicest pupils one day. Now, how's that lunch doing? I don't think we can get any further with this business until I've heard what Fiona has to say about that night; and Max, you must be thoroughly bewildered about all these people and their activities. Let's forget about Bernard for an hour and think only of our stomachs.'

' "Now good digestion wait on appetite",' said Max.

' "And health on both",' Liz answered smartly, and astounded them.

## IV

June Foster ate very little of her lunch. Her ankle still hurt; her head ached because she had cried so much; and she felt utterly wretched. Roy had spent a total of only fifteen minutes with her since she had arrived in the clinic. She could not really blame him; fancy breaking your leg on the second day of your honeymoon. But it wasn't as if the weather were fine so that he could go off ski-ing for the day. She couldn't help wondering what he was finding to do.

She thought back to the wedding on Friday, only four days ago; it was better to remember that than the humiliation which came later. She had worn a cream brocade dress and yards of tulle, and been followed down the aisle by two cousins both much slimmer and much prettier than herself. She had no real girl friends. At school she had been known as 'Podge' because of her figure. She had been good at nothing, only cooking, and that was discovered by chance when her parents could not think of anything to do with her after she left school. When Roy, whom she had known all her life, had suddenly started to take her out and generally pay her attention it had seemed the most marvellous thing that could happen. Their mothers often met; when they were children they had gone to Woolacombe for holidays at the same time. Roy, several years older, had thrown buckets of water over June and jumped on her sandcastles; she had hated him then. She blotted out the memory: lots of little boys were unkind. Their parents were delighted about the marriage. Roy's father had been killed in a motor accident when Roy was sixteen and the farm had been run by a manager until Roy was old enough to take it over.

June liked Mrs Foster, and was glad to think she would be living nearby. She was thrilled at the prospect of living in the big old house, and Roy had said that she could keep a horse, for its cost could be included in the farm accounts. June loved riding, though she was too dumpy to look good on a horse. Her father had settled a lot of money on her: she knew that the main idea was to save death duties, but she was grateful because it meant she would not be a drain on Roy but would be contributing herself to their income. She wouldn't be lonely when Roy was busy about the farm, for she would have plenty to do. She was perfectly confident about her ability to run the house well and economically, for she understood thoroughly all aspects of domestic management. It was the only thing, apart from riding, that she knew she could undertake without courting disaster. While she did her training she had lived at home, travelling back and forth to Weybridge daily on the train, inwardly thankful to be avoiding the social whirl her fellow students seemed to thrive on, though she pretended to envy them. She knew she could never cope with adventures they thought nothing of.

That was one thing about Roy. He had never alarmed her at all. Sometimes she had rather regretted his restraint. Until Friday night, at the hotel in London. She shuddered to think of it, and began to cry again; she was still snuffling into her pillow when a knock at her door announced a visitor.

It was Sam Irwin. He carried a box of chocolates and a magazine, and pretended not to notice her distress.

June quickly wiped her eyes and put on a smile. How very kind of Sam to call; she had scarcely met him, though Sue had chattered so freely about everyone at the Gentiana that June felt she knew them all.

The chocolates were delicious; June opened the box and they both began eating them. Sam inquired about her leg; then he described the fondue party and how the lights had gone out.

'Sue Carter said you played the piano and everyone danced. Roy must have enjoyed that,' she said, fishing for information.

'He danced once or twice. There's a shortage of men, so he had to,' Sam said, which was not strictly true. 'He didn't stay late.' This at least was no invention; no need to add that he had left with Fiona, who was freed by the power breakdown from her record duty.

'You've heard about poor Bernard Walker, I suppose?' Though not exactly a cheerful topic, it was at least a different one, and safer in the present context for June to talk about than her own troubles.

'Yes. What a terrible thing. How could it have happened?'

'He must have gone for a walk and slipped,' said Sam. 'He left the nightclub with Fiona.' This at any rate was a good piece of information for June to possess, in case by some mischance anyone else let fall the name of Fiona in connection with Roy. But Sam had seen Fiona later that night himself.

Unlike Bernard, Sam had a balcony to his room; he had opened his big windows and stood on it late on Saturday night watching the snow come down. His plan was to air his room, then batten the windows shut again with the radiator turned off, so that he should not wake in the night roasting gently from over-powerful heating; it was snowing too hard to leave the window open all night long. As he gazed out, sheltered by the canopy of the balcony above, in the light that streamed out from the main hotel he had seen Fiona below, wavering about on her way back to the annexe; he had seen, too, another figure join her, a stocky male who had emerged from the Gentiana's main building. A few minutes later he had heard their footsteps coming up the stairs in the annexe; they had gone on past the first floor on which the rooms of both himself and Bernard were, to Fiona's up above. A long time later Sam had heard footsteps coming down again. As far as he knew, no one else was aware that June had been abandoned for most of the second night of her honeymoon.

He knew the Cotswolds from the time that he had spent at Stratford-upon-Avon, and this gave them a safe subject to discuss. They talked about the early lambs always to be seen high up on the ridge; the stone walls and the lovely old houses with their silvery roofs; the little streams and narrow lanes; and half an hour passed pleasantly. Sam was just casting about in his mind for something else to talk about when two more visitors appeared, Sue and Jan. They carried a box of cream pastries they had bought and said they had come to tea.

'We've been swimming at the Grand,' said Sue, who was glowing.

'It's much easier than ski-ing,' Jan said. 'I don't sit down on my fat double-Dutch backside like I do on the mountain, I just give my stomach a nasty smack instead.' He rubbed his vast front. 'I cannot dive,' he added. 'But Sue is superb. What a woman she is!'

Sue smirked.

'Perhaps Roy was there too?' June suggested wistfully.

'He might have been. I didn't see him. There were quite a lot of people swimming,' Jan told her. 'Elizabeth and Dr. Grant were there. It's the only thing to do, since we cannot ski. I hope the beer won't run out before we are back in touch with the rest of the world.'

June suddenly felt a great deal better. She would ring the bell and ask the nurse to bring tea, enough for five; for surely Roy was on his way, and when he arrived he would find her popular, surrounded by her friends.

## V

Liz got a lot of sardonic amusement out of watching Sue and Jan disporting themselves in the swimming-pool. Two whales, she thought they were.

'That's unkind. Sue's not so large, she's more like a porpoise,' Patrick said. 'She swims well, doesn't she?'

Sue did, but today she was preferring to wallow playfully with Jan. Liz and Patrick swam up and down the pool briskly a few times, both keen on working off their lunch.

'I get so cross if I eat too much and can't get exercise,' said Liz.

'How do you manage in London?' Patrick asked.

'I play squash in the winter and tennis in summer,' said Liz. 'You, on the other hand, lead the indolent life of a don, and all those rowing muscles you acquired in your youth will turn to flab as you get older.'

'I hope not,' Patrick said. He hauled himself out of the pool and stood on the edge so that she could admire his physique. He kept very fit; he took a skiff out on the river several times a week when he was in Oxford, and spent part of every vacation walking or climbing. Now he executed a neat dive back into the pool and surfaced near Liz, shaking his head to toss his hair back from his eyes.

'You look so funny without your specs,' she told him. 'Rather indecent, really.'

He stretched out a hand and pressed her head firmly so that she submerged. Spluttering, she swam away from him; he would never grow up, she decided.

'Now we're going to walk to the forbidden area on the Kramms road,' he said when they were once again dry and clothed. 'I want to show you something.'

'We'll catch our deaths, walking through the snow after a swim,' she grumbled. She had hoped for an expensive, luxurious tea at the Grand.

'Not at all. You're well wrapped up. Step out smartish,' Patrick instructed.

It was much colder now, and the snow that was still falling stung their faces. As they set out, Liz tied her scarf more tightly round her head to protect her ears from the icy air. They walked through the village, past the bridge and the shops and the chair-lift terminus, and on to the fork in the road. Here the snow was deep and it was quite hard going, though there were plenty of tracks where others had been.

They reached the barrier and Patrick went past. Liz followed, and they walked on until they came to the cutting in the bank of snow at the side of the lane. Patrick led the way along it. It had been cleared since his earlier visit and only a couple of inches of new snow covered it. He stopped at the footbridge, and Liz halted, too. On the further side of the river she could see the chalet among the trees.

'Who lives there, I wonder?' she said.

'I wonder the same thing,' said Patrick.

'I'm surprised you haven't found out.'

'At the appropriate time, I will,' he replied. He moved closer to the bridge. It, too, had been cleared since the morning. A single set of tracks, lightly marking the fresh snow, led across it.

'This is where Bernard was lying, I'm convinced,' said Patrick. 'It's close to the hotel, yet away from the beaten track. Debris from here flows very quickly down to the bridge without getting unduly caught up on the way. Stay where you are a minute.' He stepped off to the side and moved a few yards down the bank; as she watched him seeking footholds Liz thought she would see his words proved in a moment; he seemed set for a second and colder swim.

Balanced on a stone off which he had kicked most of the snow, he peered into the water intently. Then he came back to her.

'What were you looking for?' she asked.

'Tell you later. Let's get back and wait for our friend to return,' said Patrick. 'Go back to the lane, will you, Liz?'

She obediently turned about. When they reached the lane he took her arm and led her further along the road towards Kramms, until they were out of sight of the cutting.

'We'll wait for a little while to see if the visitor returns,' he said. 'It may be someone we know. You stay here. If you get too cold whistle *Annie Laurie* and I'll come back.'

'Where are you going?'

'To the edge of the cutting, so that I can see if anyone's coming. When he appears I'll get out of sight, and we'll follow to see who it is.'

'Do you think it's a man?'

'Man-sized prints, or else a very large lady,' said Patrick.

'The banks of the Isis were better than this,' muttered Liz, but Patrick was already gone.

Left alone, she jumped about and stamped up and down to keep warm. Darkness would, she supposed, ultimately bring their vigil to an end. Pride would not let her admit too quickly to physical defeat, but her teeth had begun to chatter when Patrick reappeared, motioning her to keep quiet. He stood beside her, holding her hand, for a few seconds; then he gave her a little tug and they walked back along the road.

A figure moved ahead of them, indistinct through the falling snow. Patrick strode out, gaining slightly on the person in front, and Liz struggled to keep level. She was too busy clambering through the snow to watch their quarry closely, but when they got to the barrier the going was easier, for the road was clearer. One glance was all she needed to recognise Francis.

Patrick took her to Ferdy's and bought her a very large, very hot grog.

'He wasn't behaving suspiciously,' she insisted, still shivering. 'He must have seen our tracks in that cutting and leading to where we waited. He didn't even look round.'

'If he's innocent, seeing our tracks wouldn't worry him. If he's guilty we'll soon know, for he'll take some action,' said Patrick. 'You must make an effort now, old thing. Swig as much of this stuff as you like before you go back to the hotel, but carry on with your flirting just as before. We want everything normal.'

'Oh, God, how I hate you, Patrick Grant,' Liz said, emptying her glass. 'You can do your own damned detecting in future.'

## VI

That evening it grew much colder. Undaunted despite everything, Penny, who, true to her threat, had arranged a snowfight that morning with the Snopranx courier, had combined again with the rival organisation to run a dance at the Silvretta, where there was a three-piece band. She would allow no defaulters, and accordingly after dinner her flock from the Gentiana set forth.

'We may as well go,' Sue said. 'We can't go to bed at half-past eight, and there's nothing else to do.' She in fact was eager enough to obey Penny's injunction, for Jan was staying at the Silvretta and was therefore certain to be at the dance.

Even Barbara Whittaker favoured the plan.

'Let's invite Frau Hiller to come with us,' she suggested. 'I felt we should have asked her to the fondue last night. She's on her own, and I think she's lonely.'

'There are plenty of other Germans staying here,' said Freddie shortly. 'Why doesn't she pal up with some of them?'

'Perhaps she doesn't like them,' Barbara answered. 'Shared

nationality doesn't mean similar tastes. You meet all kinds of people on holiday.' She looked steadily at Freddie as she spoke, and he stared back at her boldly. This conversation took place in the dining-room, and what Liz described later to Patrick as a great moral victory had taken place, for the Whittakers had abandoned their seclusion and joined the table with the other Hickson's clients.

It was generally agreed that Frau Hiller should be included in the evening's entertainment, and Freddie was overborne. The German woman at first demurred, but she was obviously pleased at being asked, and allowed herself to be persuaded. They all walked down the road together after dinner, with Francis and Sam each giving Frau Hiller an arm.

After just a few yards, like one man, everyone stopped to gaze at the sky. It was clear and black, dotted with bright stars which none of them had seen since arriving in the mountains.

Penny sniffed the sharp air.

'It's freezing hard. It'll be fine tomorrow,' she declared.

They all stepped out, more cheerful than for days past; the cold made them catch their breaths, but all felt stimulated by the change in the atmosphere. Now the village stood out, sharply etched against the night sky, with the windows of the buildings lit by the soft glow of candles, for still the power supply was off. Only the Grand Hotel and the clinic had their own generators.

At the bridge, Roy left the party to go to the clinic. There was an amazed reaction to this.

'Don't act so surprised,' Sue said. 'It's what he should have been doing all along.' She added, *sotto voce*, to Liz, 'I doubt if Fiona will mope for long.'

She was right. Fiona, still on enforced leave from her discotheque, was soon dancing cheek-to-cheek with one of the Snopranx guests. Penny started the evening by watching her like a hawk, but when it seemed that Fiona intended to drink only shandy, and also to stick to the Snopranxter, she relaxed and began to enjoy herself.

Patrick and the professor had dined at the Silvretta, with Jan, it transpired. The band was rather good; it played catchy tunes with a rhythm that set everyone's feet tapping. The professor, bowing to her in his courtly way, invited Frau Hiller to dance; she blushed, saying she had not done such a thing for years, but she waltzed away with him.

Patrick, dancing with Liz, told her that after they had parted earlier he had sought out Fiona and taxed her with being the last person to see Bernard alive. She admitted that they had left the nightclub together. They had put on their coats in the hall of the hotel before crossing to the annexe, and got as far as the porch when Bernard said he had forgotten something and must return for it. He had not reappeared. Fiona had looked about in the hotel for him but could not find him, so she had given up.

'She met Roy, in fact,' Patrick said. 'While she was blundering about in the snow outside he arrived, looking for her. They'd had an affair of some intensity last year, and he chucked her to marry this girl. She didn't discover he was coming here till she saw Penny's list on Saturday morning, hence her getting quietly plastered and making a play for the unfortunate Bernard. Roy must have had a surprise when he saw her.'

'Where did you have this little interview with Fiona?' Liz inquired.

'In her room. Where else?'

'Well, Master Roy seems to be playing the dutiful husband tonight, anyway,' Liz commented.

'He is, indeed,' said Patrick. His tone was smug, and Liz looked at him sharply.

'You've talked to him, too,' she accused.

'I have. I flatter myself I scared the living daylights out of him,' said Patrick in an inelegant, un-donnish manner.

'But, Patrick – ' Liz's voice tailed off.

'I know what you were going to say. Why don't I mind my own business; leave it alone, and June would eventually pack it in and all that,' he said. 'But, Liz, you have an endearing way of endowing everyone else with your own disposition. I agree that someone like you would find it intolerable to be married to Roy Foster, but that girl will be quite content by the time she's got a few kids to keep her occupied. She won't even notice he's unfaithful, which he's certain to be. Soon she'll scarcely notice him at all; she'll have an agreeable ambience – nice house, healthy children, and a position in the district. She's not capable of achieving the deep relationship which you seek and need; she's just a rather silly, amiable little girl who'll turn into a rather silly, amiable mother, and be perfectly happy. If she walks out on this marriage before it goes any further, which is what you think she should do, she'll be devastated for life – marked as a failure, humiliated beyond recovery, and if she ever took another chance it would inevitably be with a second Roy.'

Liz was silent.

'How cynical you are, Patrick,' she said, after they had moved halfway round the room.

'No, just realistic,' he told her gently. 'That girl could never stand alone.'

'That's just what she will have to do, if you're right.'

'She'll have her children. That will be enough.'

'Sometimes I think you're a devil, Patrick,' Liz said. And sometimes she thought him the shrewdest person she had ever known.

'What about Bernard? If Roy and Fiona were together, that lets them both out, doesn't it?'

'Not Roy. There was an interval before he met Fiona.'

'Was it long enough?'

'Difficult to say. Fiona wasn't sure of times.'

'So what's your theory now? Have you one?'

'Yes. I know who did it,' Patrick said. 'But I can't prove it, and I don't know why.'

'So you won't tell me?'

'Not yet, Liz.'

'You could be wrong.'

'It's possible,' he conceded. 'But I don't think so.'

He would say no more. Liz's next partner, to her astonishment, was Sam; and a changed Sam he was, too, from the introverted, silent man who had been their companion for a week. By the time he and Liz had concluded an animated discussion about Shakespeare's clowns, Liz had convinced herself that he was the murderer: Bernard had threatened him for some reason; now the threat was gone, and with it had disappeared all Sam's inhibitions. For the murderer thought himself safe: she and Max were the only ones who knew of Patrick's suspicions.

Francis was rather attentive to his wife throughout the evening and did not dance with Liz at all.

# PART SIX

# Wednesday

## I

In the morning it was difficult to believe that Greutz had been the scene of sudden death, or even of the past few weeks of heavy skies and ever-falling snow. The sun rose behind the Wolfberg like a brilliant copper disc, and cast a rosy glow that crept gradually upwards over the slopes of the Schneiderhorn. Behind the great mountain the sky was blue, pale at first but darkening swiftly, and with just a few wispy clouds like cotton wool drifting across it. At breakfast in the Gentiana there were rolls once more, and during the night the electrical power had been restored to the village; things were, on the face of it, back to normal.

By half-past nine the ski-school meeting place was thrumming with eager people and a queue had already formed at the chair-lift. Everyone in the Gentiana was determined to spend the day on the Schneiderhorn; even Barbara Whittaker said she would go up and have lunch at the restaurant.

Liz decided to be very brave and ski alone. In fact, there would be plenty of people about; the mountain was likely to be smothered with activity, so that if she met with any disaster someone would be sure to notice. She saw Sue off to meet Jan in the lowest division of class three at the ski-school and lined up at the chair-lift herself. Some way in front of her, sombre in their all-black outfits, she saw the Derringtons, and as she came carefully over the shoulder of the mountain before starting down the White Run she saw Sam and Francis ahead of her; they took the left turn for the Red Run.

It was as if the events of the last few days were a hideous dream.

Liz refused to think of them, and hoped devoutly that she would not meet Patrick. Presumably the pass would be cleared today; there would be no further obstacle to his departure, and good riddance to him and his wild ideas. He was capable of dreaming it all up as a mental exercise: but not the telephone calls to England; even Patrick, trying to provoke thought, would not go that far.

And she would like to know what Francis had been doing at that chalet over the river.

She had lunch sitting in the sun outside the restaurant above the chair-lift: thick goulash soup and rough brown bread. Beside her sat a middle-aged woman from Liège; Liz talked to her in French, and felt stimulated by the exchange. After that she went down the Blue Run. Even the chair held no alarms for her today; it was the best ski-ing she had ever known, with the snow like dry powder crunching against her skis, and the *piste* well flattened, first by the snow-cat and then by the tracks of other skiers, and not a trace of ice anywhere. She dared to go fast, knees bent, relaxed in the approved style, and felt she could continue for hours.

The moment you thought that sort of thing it was time to stop. At half-past three, prudently, she took off her skis at the bottom of the run and did not go up again. Instead, she wandered through the village, which was almost deserted as everyone took advantage of their liberation.

In the big car park by the Grand Hotel, a red cross had been marked out on the ground with some sort of cloth. A group of people was gathered at the spot, gazing up the valley, and soon Liz realised the reason for it as she heard the drone of a helicopter far off. She joined the watchers, and saw two blue-clad figures holding mailbags standing at the edge of the area where the helicopter intended to land.

The machine came gliding in, its rotors cutting the silence of the sky with their sharp, clattery sound. It hovered low over its landing spot and gently came down on its runners like an awkward bird mounting its nest. The rotors continued to whir, and two men inside the machine began handing out bags of mail to their colleagues outside. Presently they got out themselves and stood talking; it seemed incredible that they could hear one another above the din of the engine. After a few minutes the pilot and his companion climbed back into the helicopter with the bags of outgoing mail, the motor accelerated, and the fragile-looking spiderly bubble rose into the air, hovered briefly once more over its temporary resting place, turned, and set off up the valley towards the wider world beyond the mountains.

The Greutz postmen went back down the road to the post office with their load, and the spectators gradually dispersed after this little burst of excitement. Liz retraced her steps through the village towards the Gentiana.

Where the road branched she stuck her skis in the snow and took the fork towards Kramms. She could hear a snow-blower working further down, and she walked on till she came to it; showers of snow came spuming up through its funnel and were added to the huge banks already piled high at the side of the road. The barrier forbidding passage along this way had been removed, and there were other walkers strolling about too; the sun had left this area and it was cold. Eventually Liz turned back again and took the narrow trench towards the footbridge. It had been swept quite clean.

There was nothing to indicate that it was a private approach; Liz took a breath and started across. The bridge swayed under her tread, and below the river swirled, still carrying twigs and debris down to the village. Halfway across she paused and looked downstream; the covered wooden bridge was not far away, though the distance by road was several hundred yards. Patrick's theory was tenable.

A path on the further bank climbed up into the trees. Liz followed it, and soon came to the chalet, an old one that must have been built long before the war. Huge eaves covered with snow framed the windows like beetle brows. A sign hung out: *Zimmer.* It was a guest house. Had Francis been researching accommodation for another year? It seemed unlikely. Barbara was hardly the sort of woman to enjoy humbler rooms than those at the Gentiana. Wildly seeking a reason for his visit, Liz remembered his daughter : perhaps in some way it was connected with her.

The theory was unsatisfactory, but Liz could not think of a better one, nor could she devise an excuse to knock on the door of the chalet and pose some question which might lead her to the true answer. In any case, her German was not equal to such a conversation. Before someone saw her loitering about outside, she turned back.

## II

Hilda Derrington shot past her husband as they went down the Red Run towards the end of the afternoon. She sped over the hanging bridge and skidded to a halt on the slope above the Gentiana, pushed her sticks into the snow and waited for Freddie to catch her up. This was only one of a great many things she did better than he.

'Well? Has she given in yet?' she demanded when he drew level.

'Has who given in? I don't know what you're talking about.' Freddie wore goggles to protect his eyes from the sun; Hilda could not see his expression as they faced one another.

'Oh, you do bore me,' she sighed. 'It's the same wherever we go. Always you get the idea of making a big conquest. But this time you had some help, some threat. I know you managed to frighten Barbara Whittaker.' She laughed, mockingly. 'Silly woman. I could tell her it's just bluster. What happened in Malta? I'm very certain you had no more luck with her then than here.'

'There's a painter fellow out there,' Freddie said, sulkily. 'She meets him every year.'

'Ah ha. And her husband knows all about it, so she doesn't really mind if you do tell him, except that it would be uncivilised if it all came into the open. You'll never learn, will you?'

'It wasn't like that,' Freddie muttered.

'You're like a little boy, begging for sweets,' Hilda jeered at him. 'It amuses me to watch you, but not when you make a fool of me as well as yourself. Locking me into the bathroom was so childish. As if that would give you time enough. Goodness knows you need all night when things are at their best.'

Freddie slid forward on his skis, raising a stick and glowering, but Hilda only laughed at him.

'That's right. Get good and angry, if you can,' she said. 'I'd like to see you manage something.' Slowly she glided away from him, starting down the slope towards the hotel, not glancing back. Just as slowly, Freddie followed.

## III

Fiona and Penny sat in the sun outside the restaurant at Obergreutz having a hot lemonade before going down for the last time. Already shadows were falling across the slopes below as the light faded; the sun, fiery gold, was low in the sky behind them. Their smooth faces shone with sun-tan oil, and their hair, long and glossy, the auburn and the blonde, was like silk in the bright light.

'I'm getting out as soon as there's transport,' Fiona said. 'Sorry to let you down and all that, Penny, but I can't stand seeing him now, and there's over another week to go. Weird, isn't it? All of a sudden I hate him.' She shuddered. 'It must have been a sort of madness that got into us, starting up again, and then when June had that accident it was all so easy – '

'He can't be very nice, Fiona,' Penny said. 'After all, he did marry her. And the way he chucked you with scarcely a word was pretty heartless.'

'Niceness has nothing to do with it,' Fiona said bitterly. She looked at Penny. 'You think I'm terrible, don't you?'

'I think you're very stupid,' Penny said firmly. 'I just don't understand what you can see in a person like that. I've had some pretty rum customers on my tours before, but he wins the prize for all-out callousness. Fancy bringing June on a ski-ing honeymoon when she'd never done it before.'

'Where else can you go in the winter?'

'Oh, Tenerife. Or get married in the summer.'

'He couldn't afford to wait,' Fiona said in a harsh voice. 'Her father settled a lot of money on her. He's heavily in debt.'

'And you fell for a man like that?'

'I told you, niceness has nothing to do with it,' Fiona snapped. 'He could just turn me on in a way no one else ever has. But never again. I'm over it.' She shivered. There was something strange about June's accident, she knew: Roy should never have taken her up the Schneiderhorn that day; it didn't make sense. But she also knew he was totally ruthless when anything stood in his way.

'Well, I'm glad I'm not like you,' said Penny, standing up. She stretched, and fastened the zip of her jacket. 'I like my pleasures simple. Come on, time to go back, it's getting cold.'

## IV

Seeing the sunshine, Max abandoned Marlowe.

'I have merely to check some references,' he said to Patrick. 'Let us have a long, healthy day on the mountain, for the pass will surely be cleared today and we shall have to return to the claims of our pupils.'

Accordingly they set off, leaving the breakfast for Helga to wash up, for after a telephone call to Kramms the professor seemed confident she would return during the day. They spent the morning on the summit of the Schneiderhorn, using the twin anchor drag from Obergreutz and the interlacing runs that connected with it. It was glorious up there in the thin, clear air; Patrick could feel it cold in his lungs. Round them ranged the mighty peaks of the mountains, jagged against the blue, and marked starkly by the dark lines of ravines and other surfaces too sheer to hold the snow.

'Everyone should be compelled to spend at least a day a year in these regions,' Patrick said. 'For the good of his soul.'

'It does bring home our littleness,' Max said. 'You find the mountains uplifting?'

'Spiritually and physically,' Patrick said.

They lunched at Obergreutz, sitting out on the terrace in the sunshine. It was crowded; everyone seemed to be there, people of all nationalities, many of whom Patrick had never seen before in his peregrinations around the village.

'One would not think that Greutz could hold so many people,' he observed, when he and Max had managed to find somewhere to sit with their bowls of stew.

'They don't all come from Greutz. Some are from Kramms, and the little villages at the other side,' said the professor. 'We'll go down to Kramms after lunch. It's a pleasant run, and the trip back by cable-car will be very agreeable on a day like this.'

'Right,' Patrick agreed. 'Is it difficult?'

'Not as hard as the Red Run back to Greutz. It gets icy sometimes under the trees, but today it will be beginner's stuff,' said Max, twinkling at Patrick through his spectacles.

Patrick saw Liz across the terrace; she made no sign of having noticed him, and he knew she did not want to talk to him. He did not think he needed her help to fit together the final pieces of the puzzle. Everyone else whom he had met in the village was up there, too; he saw Sue and Jan among a class of about sixteen others, mostly, girls, who were being chivvied along by a bronzed *lehrer* who punctuated his instructions with flattering quips as they stem-christied inexpertly over the wide plateau below the restaurant. Hilda and Freddie Derrington lunched with Penny and Fiona; then they took the anchor drag up higher, leaving the two girls alone. Francis Whittaker and Sam Irwin were ski-ing together; Patrick and the professor had met them on the summit; at lunch they were joined by Barbara and Frau Hiller, who had come up on the chair to enjoy the superb panorama spread out around them and seemed content now to sit in the sun indefinitely, watching the skiers. Roy appeared, apparently alone; he sat on the steps, for want of a free seat, eating the packed lunch he had brought up from the Gentiana and with a big tankard of beer; he was hidden from Fiona and Penny by the side of the restaurant building. It was a colourful scene, with the whiteness of the snow splashed with the bright colours of the skiers' clothing, the gay flags flying on the restaurant, and the clumps of skis, blue, yellow, red and black, standing upright in the snow.

'Let's see if Whittaker and Irwin will come down to Kramms with us,' Patrick suggested, when he and Max were ready to go. The professor was very willing, and the other two men thought the plan excellent. Francis was familiar with the run, but Sam, like Patrick, modestly wondered if he could manage it.

'If I can, you can,' Patrick assured him.

They all had another beer together before setting off.

'It's amazing how much you can drink with no effects at all when you're ski-ing all day,' Sam remarked.

'The altitude is conveniently dehydrating in its effect,' the professor agreed. He finished his drink, stood up, and began to put on his skis, knocking the packed snow from the bottom of his boots with his sticks. He led the way down to Kramms, and Francis, as the next best skier, came at the end. It was indeed a lovely run, starting off with a gently undulating slope above the tree-line and eventually dropping to a narrow *piste* that wound through the forest, crossed to a stream, and presently emerged into the open fields leading into Kramms. They debated having another beer in the village before going up again, but decided not to put the drying effects of the thin air to the test so strongly until later. It was only a short walk from the end of the *piste* to the cable-car, and a cabin was waiting when they reached the station; soon, whining and whirring, it began the ascent back to Obergreutz. The valley fell away rapidly as they were swept up the mountain and they were able to pick out various landmarks below.

Patrick pointed to a chalet visible among the trees near the river bank.

'Isn't that the Chalet Edelweiss?' he asked. 'A widow, Frau Weber, runs it as a guest house, doesn't she, Max?'

'Yes, indeed,' replied the professor. 'It is sometimes used by travel agents sending out parties to study wild flowers. Many English people come there in the summer.'

'You know Frau Weber, don't you, Whittaker?' Patrick went on.

Francis looked somewhat taken aback. Then he answered, calmly enough.

'Yes. Her family hid me for several months during the war. I always call to see her when I come to Greutz.'

'What happened to her husband?' Patrick inquired.

'He was at the Russian front during the war, but he survived,' Max said. 'He was killed in a climbing accident some years ago. Frau Weber has a son, a fine boy, a great comfort to his mother. He has just qualified as an architect. I am correct, am I not?' he asked Francis.

'Perfectly correct,' Francis agreed.

'I supplied a reference as to the young man's character some years ago,' the professor continued.

'Did you? I never knew that,' said Francis.

'It was before the boy went to the university,' the professor said. 'I had just taken up my appointment at Innsbruck. Previously I was attached to Salzburg.' He looked at Francis thoughtfully. 'A fine young man,' he repeated slowly. 'Very much like his father in appearance. A son to be proud of.'

Patrick had hitherto considered himself immune to surprise, but this conversation astounded him. He knew that Max had held his present post for eight years; the boy would have been seventeen or eighteen when he went to university, so that he must have been born in 1944 or thereabouts, after Francis had finally escaped. No doubt Herr Weber was not the only returning warrior who had to face such a situation. He saw that Francis meant to answer the professor, and decided to divert Sam, who was very astute.

'You've enjoyed today's ski-ing?' he asked him.

'Very much,' Sam said. 'It's amazing how quickly one forgets all that bad weather. Two or three days like this make the whole thing worth while. It was a great extravagance for me coming on this holiday, but I was ill before Christmas and I wanted to be at my best for this new production next month. I missed a great chance once before through ill-health. I did quite a lot of ski-ing when I was a student and always enjoyed it.'

'You went to drama school?'

'No. I read history. I started acting with the university dramatic society,' Sam said. 'I was a schoolmaster for a long time; then I decided to take the plunge.'

'Brave of you,' said Patrick.

'Well, there was only myself to consider. I had no family dependent on me,' Sam said.

The cable car arrived, swaying, at its platform on the mountain side, and when they disembarked from the scarlet cabin they found Barbara and Frau Hiller waiting to greet them.

'We thought you must be having another beer in Kramms,' said Barbara. 'We wondered whether to come down to find you, but we decided you'd be on the way up as we went down.'

'We came straight back, darling,' Francis told her. 'Not a drop passed our lips.'

Patrick marvelled anew at the nature of marriage; what an odd bargan these two had clearly struck: her summer trips to Malta; his winter visits to Greutz following the death of the man who had acted as a father to his son. No doubt in Dorset their double-harness worked efficiently; Francis looked after Barbara's property, and she took care of his daughter. At least he had not washed his hands of Frau Weber after he moved out of her life. By contrast, how much more restful was the existence of a bachelor, free from emotional entanglements. Occasionally Patrick wondered if he were missing something valuable, but situations such as this one made him thankful not to be at risk.

They walked back towards the restaurant and the chair-lift, the men with their skis over their shoulders, and the two women unencumbered except for the shoulder-bags each carried.

'We'd better go straight down and have tea in the village,' Barbara said. 'It's getting cold.'

'Yes, the sun is setting,' Frau Hiller said.

'We'll see you later, then,' Barbara said to the men. 'Shall we meet at the Silvretta?'

It was agreed. Frau Hiller and Barbara went off to take the chair down, and the men put on their skis. They decided to take the Red Run. This time Francis took the lead; Sam went next;

and Patrick followed. There were a lot of people going down for the last run of the day, and it was necessary to keep a good look-out to avoid collisions in the narrow parts of the *piste*. As he started off, Patrick glanced back to see if Max were following; he had finished adjusting his skis and was putting on his gloves ready to start. Once or twice during the trip down he looked back again, but he could not see Max behind him; however, he was the strongest skier and the least likely to come to grief, in spite of his extra years. Francis crossed the hanging bridge and stopped some way below it, above the Gentiana; Sam joined him, triumphant because he had ski-ed well and held the pace; then Patrick reached them. They waited.

'Where's the professor?' Sam asked at last. 'He's taking an awful long time.'

They went on waiting. There was no sign of Max.

'Let's ask someone if they've seen him,' Francis said. He stopped the next man down and spoke to him, but he had seen no bearded man in any trouble on the run.

'Perhaps he didn't hear which way we were coming and has taken another route?' Sam suggested. 'He may be in the Silvretta.'

'Let's go and see,' said Patrick.

Max was not in the Silvretta, and neither were Barbara and Frau Hiller. Jan and Sue, who were, had seen none of them.

'He must be at the top still. I'll go up,' said Patrick.

'I'll come with you,' Francis said.

'Don't bother, unless you want another run.'

'Of course I'll come. Anyway, another run down would round off the day nicely.'

'If you'll excuse me, I won't chance it,' Sam said. 'I feel a bit stiff. Besides, I'm not as good as you two, and I might get in the way.'

'Right. Perhaps you'd wait for Barbara and tell her what's happened,' said Francis.

Sam agreed and sat down with Sue and Jan. Patrick and Francis went back to the chair-lift terminus. When they reached it they found Barbara standing there, looking anxious.

'Frau Hiller hasn't come down,' she said. 'She wanted me to

go ahead of her, and when I looked back she wasn't on the next chair. I thought perhaps she'd simply missed it, but there was a big gap before the next person. I was wondering whether to go up again and look for her. Maybe she's been taken ill.'

'We'll look for her,' said Patrick. 'We're going up again.'

Francis cast a swift glance at him. He had not mentioned Max.

'Sam's waiting for you in the Silvretta, darling,' Francis said. 'You join him. We'll see what's happened. Maybe she felt giddy or something.'

'I hope she's all right. She was very quiet all afternoon, but she seemed quite well. I suggested coming down earlier, before you all got back from Kramms, but she wanted to stay on the top.'

'Well, don't worry. If she's feeling groggy we'll see she gets down safely,' Francis said.

'All right,' said Barbara, but she still looked doubtful.

'We'd better get straight up,' said Francis to Patrick, moving out to the platform.

'Yes.' Patrick followed him.

'Off you go, darling,' Francis called to Barbara. He looked at Patrick. 'I know there's something going on, but I'm not sure what,' he said. 'Explanations later.'

'That's right,' Patrick said.

It was impossible to communicate throughout the journey to Obergreutz, and Patrick sat fuming with impatience in his chair. Francis, in front, seemed to be admiring the scenery. There were only a few descending passengers; Patrick scrutinised them intently in case Frau Hiller or the professor were among them. When they reached the top there was no one about; the sun had sunk low and it was very cold.

'Not a sign of them,' Francis said. He lifted his skis on to his shoulder. 'We'd better try the restaurant. If she isn't feeling well, that's where Frau Hiller will be.'

He pushed open the door of the restaurant and they went in. There were just a handful of skiers and a group of *lehrers* waiting till the last tourists had gone down, before they made their own descents to see that the runs were clear. Frau Hiller and the professor were nowhere to be seen.

'Max is well known here. If we ask the *lehrers* they'll know who we're looking for,' said Patrick.

'I know most of the *lehrers*. There's Fritz Gruber, I'll ask him,' said Francis.

Fritz Gruber, one of the older instructors, with a lined, weather-beaten face, said at once that he had seen Professor Klocker and a lady travelling up on the anchor drag together, some time before. A lady no longer young, he expanded, upon being questioned further, and by signs he indicated Frau Hiller's pear-shaped figure. He had noticed her because she seemed a little nervous on her skis, and he had not seen her ski-ing earlier.

'We'd better go up. The drag hasn't stopped yet,' said Patrick. 'Come on, hurry.'

'I suppose you know what all this is about?' said Francis.

'Not altogether. You may be able to fill in some of the gaps,' said Patrick. They strapped their skis on quickly and stepped up the slope to the foot of the drag. The attendant, who was expecting only the *lehrers* to go up at this late hour, was in two minds about turning them back, but Francis spoke to him in German, with a quick jest about making the best of the weather, and he waved them on.

'This is the sort of moment where one of us does a fool thing and breaks a leg,' said Francis grimly as they were borne upwards, their skis parallel, running in tracks already cut by the day's activities. 'Now come on. Fill me in. That professor of yours is a smart operator, isn't he? I suppose you're another. What's behind it all? It's to do with Walker in some way, I imagine. That's the only possible explanation.'

'Indirectly. I don't know how Frau Hiller fits into it. I'm guessing about that part,' Patrick said. 'You know her quite well, don't you? How did you meet her?'

'She spoke to us. She arrived last Wednesday, and on Thursday she made some remark about the weather and said she wanted to practise her English. She seemed very shy. Barbara is always glad to find someone to talk to when we're here, as she doesn't ski; she was quite willing to make friends, and when we found Frau Hiller played bridge it all seemed very easy. She's a nice old thing. Her

German's funny, though. Absolutely fluent, but a bit like her English, pedantic and old-fashioned. Her English isn't so marvellous but she understands everything.'

'I hadn't noticed that about her German,' said Patrick, chagrined. 'My own isn't good enough to make such fine distinctions.'

'I think it is pretty good, if I may say so,' said Francis handsomely. 'Your accent is better than mine. I speak the local sort of German, rather rough.'

'Frau Hiller came only last Wednesday, you say. How did she arrive?'

'She came in a taxi. She'd had a bad journey and went straight to bed on Wednesday evening. She had some private travelling arrangement, she wasn't with any agency.'

While they talked Patrick was once again watching the descending skiers closely, but now he knew that neither Frau Hiller nor the professor would be among them.

Thinking aloud, he said, 'Max could have arranged for someone to leave a pair of skis and boots up here for her. He can't have been working this alone. Maybe Helga helped him. Or his ex-pianist friend in Kramms.'

'I'm not with you at all, I'm afraid,' said Francis.

They reached the top of the drag and flung the hook away behind them, ski-ing from it. Then they stood on the crest of the mountain, staring ahead. There was no one in sight, but there were ski tracks leading off in every direction. Patrick himself had been all over this area with Max that morning. Up here the ski-ing was easy; it was possible to pick a gentle route not difficult for someone who was out of practice.

Then they heard it, in the distance, to the west of them, before the setting sun: a helicopter's engine. Francis, the former soldier, saw it first.

'It's coming in to land,' he said.

It was a long way from them, above a bowl in the mountains, away from any connecting links. Max must have had a job to get her there through the deep snow, Patrick thought; he would have had to cut tracks first for her to follow in.

'What was she interested in? Did she talk about her hobbies? Frau Hiller, I mean,' he demanded suddenly.

'Oh, knitting. She was making that rather drab sweater. Barbara joked about it behind her back. The wool was so poor, she said. She seemed to know a lot about agriculture, wanted to know how the Derringtons fed their mink and had a wide theoretical knowledge of British wild flowers. Rather odd for a native of Frankfurt.'

'I don't think she is a native of Frankfurt,' said Patrick. He added slowly, 'Max must have been worried to risk getting her out like this. I suppose he could have carried her, at a pinch. He's fit for his age and such a good skier. Would you reckon he could do that?' he asked Francis.

'If pushed, yes. You or I would find it tough going, but I would guess he could manage it in an emergency.'

The helicopter note had changed.

'It's down,' Francis said. 'It's somewhere behind that little peak.' He pointed into the distance. The hump of a small mountain hid the helicopter from their sight. Almost at once the engine note picked up again and the machine rose into the air; they saw it hover for a moment; then it faded rapidly away towards the south-west, and Switzerland.

'There was a conference of scientists in Munich last week,' Patrick said. 'Not in Frankfurt, in Munich. A colleague of mine from Oxford was attending it. Ecological experts from all over the world were coming to it. By now they'll all be back at home again, except for one woman.'

Francis stared.

'And the professor?' he asked at last. 'What about him?'

'He'll have made his plans,' Patrick said.

There would not be another mistake.

# PART SEVEN

# Thursday

## I

PATRICK spent the night in the professor's study reading his Marlowe manuscript. He had sent Helga to bed at midnight, when there was still no news of Max. She was distraught, and mystified; his theory that she had been involved in the disappearance of Frau Hiller was perforce discarded; the old pianist in Kramms must have been Max's accomplice.

Early in the evening, Patrick and Lin had gone to Frau Hiller's room at the Gentiana; they had found it almost bare. There was a pile of paperbacks stamped with the hotel's address, all in English, and a cheap suitcase which contained a few garments, quite new and locally bought. Tidily rolled up in a drawer was the knitting, and an envelope addressed to Frau Scholler which held enough money to pay for the room Frau Hiller had occupied just for a week.

After Helga had gone reluctantly to bed, Patrick switched on the radio: he heard the announcement that a woman scientist had failed to return to her own country after an international conference in Munich; she was an ecological expert. Her present whereabouts were not revealed but it was thought she was on her way to the United States.

Between the pages of Max's book another text was fixed, in an envelope addressed to Patrick. He had read it several times, and also the manuscript in its entirety, by the time the chair-lift started down early in the morning, bringing Max's dead, frozen body back to Greutz.

## II

'But why did he have to kill Bernard?' Liz asked. Another sunny day had passed, not as fine as the one before, for there had been a few flurrying snow showers, but they had not amounted to much and nothing had prevented the arrival of officials by helicopter to unravel the mystery of Max's last hours. There had been no snowfall in the night to obliterate the tracks on the mountain showing how the professor had climbed and ski-ed back to Obergreutz from the point where Frau Hiller had been taken off by helicopter. By the time he reached Obergreutz it must have been very late: the chair-lift had long ago ceased, and the restaurant had closed when the last cable-car left for Kramms at nine o'clock. Because they had been cut off for so many days, the family who ran the restaurant had gone down to Kramms, so there would have been no one to hear Max if he had knocked. He had gone to the chair-lift station, perhaps intending to ski down in the fitful light of the waning moon, but needing a rest first. His skis were still on his feet, but he had automatically closed the bar of the chair he sat in; there he had been, rigidly in position, when the lift had started early in the morning, killed by a heart attack, Dr Wesser thought.

'Bernard overheard Max and Frau Hiller talking on Saturday night, in the ski-room at the Gentiana,' Patrick answered Liz. He tapped a paper in his hand. 'It's all in here.'

'He left that for you?'

'It was in his manuscript. He knew I'd look at what he'd been working on, and find it.'

'So he never meant to come back?'

'Shall we say that he foresaw he might not have the strength to manage it.'

'But it was an accident – Max's death? He didn't take anything, pills of some sort?'

'I think it was an accident at that point. He intended to come back and clear up the position about Bernard, once his task was done.'

'But how did you connect Max and Bernard? There was no link between them.'

'On Tuesday morning after Bernard's body had been found I went to that cutting in the snow by the river bank leading to the Chalet Edelweiss, and saw Bernard's glasses in the water. Later that day, when you and I went there together, they had gone. And when you and I came to the chalet for lunch I knew Max had been out, although he never said he had.'

'How?'

'I'd cleared the snow from the path before breakfast. It continued to snow during the morning, though not heavily. There was about an inch or so of new snow when I left that morning. When you and I got back together at lunch-time there were no tracks at all. There should have been traces of my footsteps earlier; it wasn't blowing, and what snow had fallen should have left hollows where I had walked. Also the amount of snow covering the path was very slight, showing it had been cleared again.'

'But Max didn't know Bernard had been found.'

'He was with me on the balcony when we saw the commotion by the bridge. I said I would go down and see what it was about and then call on you. He could easily have found out what had happened – he must have guessed. He knew I'd be gone some time and he took a chance on meeting someone involved with Bernard on the way. None of his local acquaintances would have wondered at his presence in the village.'

'But how did he know Bernard's glasses weren't on his face?'

'He didn't, specifically. He went to see if there was anything indicating that Bernard had been lying near the river at that point, and saw the glasses, just as I did.'

'But he was a nice man, a plus person. Why do such a terrible thing? Killing Bernard was surely out of character. He wanted to get Frau Hiller away for humanitarian reasons.'

'He didn't mean to kill Bernard. He didn't know who he was at first, remember. Frau Hiller – it's simpler to go on calling her that – wasn't the first person he'd helped to escape. Other people were involved in the business, he was just a link, but he'd kept people hidden in Greutz before, in a hotel, where they wouldn't be noticed among the ordinary visitors in the way that a guest staying with Max would be conspicuous. She was safe here when we were all cut off, as long as no one discovered who she was. Don't forget the telephone was working – anyone breaking her disguise could have made contact with the world outside. It's the sort of thing any newspaper would have loved, and would have paid well for – imagine if that wastrel Derrington had known about it, for example. In fact the one person who did discover it was about the most harmless – and he probably didn't understand what they were talking about anyway, since he knew very little German. If the news had leaked out before she was safely in some sort of sanctuary, the Communists might have managed to snatch her back again. She's a pretty good prize.'

Patrick paused to collect his thoughts. Then he continued.

'This thing was all planned a long time ago. Frau Hiller had to find an opportunity to get out from behind the Iron Curtain. Her instructions were to make friends with any English people she might find in the hotel, and I was invited to lecture to Max's students at this time so that he could ask me here, and fraternise more easily with the English community. The fact that you happened to be here, and I was keen to see you, simply played into his hands. Someone else got Frau Hiller out of Munich and brought her here; Max then had to make contact with her.'

'He used you,' Liz said.

'He did.' This was a point Patrick was trying not to dwell on in his mind.

'He talked to Frau Hiller in the ski-room, telling her he'd get her out by helicopter as soon as he could. The bad weather upset their plans, they'd intended that she should lie low for only a few days. She went back into the hotel by the inside route, and Max left by the outer door. As he did so, he came upon Bernard hiding in a corner. He'd gone there presumably to dodge Fiona. Max, almost as a reflex, hit Bernard with his torch. Afterwards he recognised him as the man we'd met in the hall of the hotel, who'd said, *"Entschuldigen sie,"* and so might have understood all they'd said. At first Max thought of bringing him up to the chalet, letting me into the plan and holding Bernard a prisoner until it was all safely over. Then he realised that he had hit him too hard and he was in a bad way. Bernard had his galoshes on – even with Fiona sticking to him like a leech he'd put them on – and Max removed them and put them in the cloakroom. Then he put Bernard on a sledge and pulled him down to the cutting. It was the nearest place where he could dump Bernard without being seen, and where he would soon be covered with snow.'

'It was dreadfully callous.'

'Yes. But he had killed before, during the years after the war when he first became involved in this kind of thing. He probably thought subconsciously that anyone skulking like that late at night in the ski-room was expendable if Frau Hiller could be saved.'

'But where were you while all this was going on? You and he left together.'

'He came back with me and waited till I'd gone to bed. Then he slipped out again. I didn't hear him go. If he'd met anyone, or if I had heard him, he'd have pretended he'd left something at the Gentiana, and come back for it.'

'And all the time Bernard wouldn't have understood a word they'd said.'

'No. But he'd have thought their meeting mysterious, at the very least.'

'But who was the professor to decide that Bernard's life was less valuable than Frau Hiller's?'

'Exactly, Liz. But it's true, you know, that great characters don't hide at midnight, wearing galoshes. Nevertheless, Max knew that would be my argument, and that I'd hound him as soon as I realised he was responsible. So he had to speed things up and get Frau Hiller away quickly. I trusted him to the extent that I thought he must have a very good reason for being so ruthless. I gave him time. I didn't know why he had done it, you see, until last night.'

'It's an extraordinary business,' Liz said.

'It was an obsession. His wife was Jewish, remember. She was arrested by the S.S. early in the war. Max knew the whereabouts of some other Jews who were in hiding – they lived in Vienna then – and he was persuaded to betray them in exchange for his wife and daughter's safety. Of course it was a trick. The other Jews were taken, but Max's wife and the baby were never seen again. Max has been trying ever since to avenge their deaths – and salve his own conscience.'

'But Patrick, even if Bernard had understood what they were talking about, surely Frau Hiller would have been safe? This is Austria, not Russia.'

'We're pretty near the Iron Curtain. Even with all Hickson's clients guarding her night and day I would think the Communists might have got her back – or killed her. They've probably got an agent or two not far away.'

'What happens now?'

'We do nothing to indicate Bernard's death was not an accident. The autopsy will show he struck his head. Let Max's reputation stay intact. And I'll see his book through the press, as he has asked.'

After a while Liz said, 'Perhaps this will stop you interfering another time, Patrick.'

'No, Liz. Bernard had a mother, after all. He might have had a whole family depending on him. His life was his, to live fully, and Max agreed with that. He meant to face the consequences when he returned. As all obsessions tend to, his got out of hand in the end.'

'What about his scholarship?'

'His academic integrity, you mean? That was total. After all, it was one of the things he grew obsessed about – freedom, and the right to express opinions. He developed his work so that he became known internationally, because in that way he could travel and make contact with people who might be seeking freedom. He met Frau Hiller six years ago. It took her all this time to find a legitimate way of leaving her own country.'

'I can't believe it,' Liz sighed. 'I thought it must be one of the others – Freddie, for instance.'

'Or your precious Francis, who was blameless – a pillar, in fact, at the end.' Patrick debated whether to tell her about Frau Weber and the Edelweiss. Because of Bernard's death she had avoided deeper involvement, but she might go on wondering. He recounted, very concisely, the conversation in the cable-car.

Liz listened without interrupting. When he had done she was silent for a time.

'You see, it is best to run away,' she said.

*Other Arrow Books of interest:*

## GRAVE MATTERS

### Margaret Yorke

A sudden flurry of movement in the Athenian twilight. A half-stifled scream. The full impact of a fatal fall.

Dr Patrick Grant had seen the whole thing – but even he couldn't be sure that he had witnessed a murder.

Then came a second 'accident', in almost identical circumstances. And Grant's suspicions turned to certainty.

Who would want to murder two apparently harmless old ladies? And why? The answer lay in a quiet Hampshire village – where a ruthless killer was already preparing to claim another victim.

## DEAD IN THE MORNING

### Margaret Yorke

If ever there was a candidate for murder, it was old Mrs Ludlow. Arrogant, cruel, demanding, she dominated every aspect of her children's lives.

So when the housekeeper at Pantons was found dead, everyone – including the police – assumed that the fatal dose of drugs had been intended for her employer.

Dr Patrick Grant, Oxford don and amateur sleuth, knew they were wrong. And he could prove it – but only at the risk of incriminating an innocent person . . .

# SHAKE HANDS FOR EVER

## Ruth Rendell

Robert Hathall brings his irascible mother to Kingsmarkham, hoping that the relationship between her and Angela, his second wife, will mellow. But when they arrive, Angela is not at the station to meet them; nor it seems is there any sign of her at Robert's cottage – not until Mrs Hathall goes upstairs and finds the strangled body on a bed.

From the outset, Chief Inspector Wexford feels uneasy about the case – there are altogether too many loose ends. Who was the other woman in Robert's life? Could Angela really have been the victim of an intruder? And whose was the strange handprint in the bath?

Wexford's suspicions lead him to London – and to a startlingly bizarre turn of events.

# SILENT WITNESS

It was a small boy who found the body, half-submerged beneath the black, icy waters of the alpine river.

The search parties returned wearily from the snow-bound ski slopes, the hotel guests talked brightly of other things, and another holiday tragedy began to slip quietly into the past.

But Dr Patrick Grant saw the tell-tale clues on the waterlogged corpse and he knew that Bernard Walker's death had been no accident.

Also in Arrow by Margaret Yorke:

GRAVE MATTERS

DEAD IN THE MORNING

MORTAL REMAINS